UNLEASHED

UNLEASHED

GORDON KORMAN

Scholastic Press • New York

Library of Congress Control Number: 2014947735

ISBN 978-0-545-70935-4

10 9 8 7 6 5 4 3 2 1   15 16 17 18 19

Printed in the U.S.A.   23
First edition, January 2015

The text type was set in ITC Century.
Book design by Elizabeth B. Parisi

32003 4687

For Robbie Twible, Superfan

The silver mouse was in full flight down Honeybee Street, body angled into the wind, round ears flattened by the force of sheer speed. The hood ornament's long rodent tail trailed straight toward the windshield of the battered red truck.

The truck backfired, and Ben Slovak jumped a foot in the air.

Griffin Bing laughed. "What's with you, Ben? That thing backfires every day, and every day you hit the moon. When are you going to get used to it?"

"When is Ralph going to get a new truck?" Ben countered testily. "Ferret Face doesn't like loud noises, you know. It gives him a nervous stomach."

A furry head emerged from the collar of Ben's shirt. From his pocket, Ben took out a thin slice of pepperoni and offered it to the little creature. The food disappeared in a heartbeat.

"Ralph should have a fleet of limousines for all the money he's charged us to get rid of the spiders in our basement!" complained Logan Kellerman. "My parents say he's the most overpriced exterminator on Long Island."

Griffin, Ben, Logan, and their friends Savannah Drysdale, Pitch Benson, and Melissa Dukakis watched as the exterminator's vehicle rolled on past them.

A faint bark sounded in the distance.

"Uh-oh." Savannah turned to look behind her. Everyone else turned, too.

It began as a tiny dot two blocks back but grew at an alarming rate. The bark grew, too, swelling to a roar.

Shy Melissa agitated her head, causing her curtain of hair to part. Her beady eyes widened. "Is that—?"

"Luthor!" exclaimed Savannah in a scolding voice. "Stop this instant!"

Savannah may have been Long Island's premier dog whisperer, but her words had no effect on the giant, galloping Doberman. Luthor was intent only on the truck. He hurtled up the street, all one hundred fifty pounds of him, in a determined bid to overtake the exterminator.

Spying the dog in hot pursuit, the driver stomped on the gas and pulled away. It only made Luthor run harder.

Now Savannah was running, too, her book bag bouncing behind her. *"Luthor—Sweetie—come back!"*

"Shouldn't we help her?" asked Melissa in a small voice.

"Count me out," Ben replied, nervously stroking Ferret Face's little head. "If Luthor thinks he can take down a whole truck, just imagine what he could do to one of us!"

"We're going to be late for school," Pitch warned. "If you have a bad attendance record, they don't let you try out for sports."

"I thought they already told you that the wrestling team is boys only," said Logan.

Pitch was tight-lipped. "That's sexist."

"Maybe so," said Griffin, "but it's also the rules."

Pitch stuck out her jaw. "The team is supposed to have the best wrestlers in the school. I pity the poor guy who thinks he can wrestle me and win."

No one disputed this. Pitch was the most talented athlete at Cedarville Middle School, thanks to the skills and conditioning she had acquired from her rock-climbing family. The only thing more painful than wrestling her would be arguing with her when she was sure she was right. She had already been kept off the all-male football team. Wrestling seemed to be next.

The five of them continued along the street, heading toward the end of the block and the cut-through that led to Cedarville Middle School. After a few minutes, they caught up to Savannah. She had hold of Luthor by the collar and was scolding him gently but firmly.

"I don't know what's gotten into you. You've never chased cars before. You could have been hurt, or even killed! What would I do without my Sweetie?"

Luthor looked contrite. But when a distant backfire sounded, he perked up and seemed to want to run off again.

"Absolutely not!" Savannah snapped. "I'm taking you home, and I expect you to stay there. Is that understood?"

Ben leaned in to the group. "She knows he's a dog, right?"

"Big talk from the guy with a weasel in his shirt," Pitch tossed back.

They all knew it wasn't the same thing. Luthor was a pet; Ferret Face was a medical service animal. Ben suffered from narcolepsy, a sleep disorder. It was the little ferret's job to provide a wake-up nip whenever he felt his owner beginning to nod off.

"You guys go without me," Savannah called. "I'll get my mom to write me a note. This is an emergency." She started back down Honeybee, leading her Doberman by the collar.

The rest of them continued to the end of the street and the cut-through to school. Griffin was the first to notice that something was different. The last house on the block had an odd triangular lawn abutting the wooded area. Now, on the grass, blocking the access to the cut-through, stood a wooden sawhorse. Against it leaned a hand-painted sign:

PRIVATE PROPERTY
NO TRESPASSING
THIS MEANS YOU

Ben frowned. "Why would Mrs. Martindale block the shortcut?"

"Maybe it's a joke," suggested Logan.

Griffin shook his head. "Mrs. Martindale never jokes."

Pitch looked exasperated. "It's a sign, not the Great Wall of China. Go around it."

"It says 'no trespassing,'" Logan pointed out.

"We're not trespassing; we're just passing through." She stepped around the sawhorse and began to cross the triangular strip of lawn.

"Hey!"

Running across the grass was a short, wiry man in his forties with dark hair and black, staring eyes. With both hands, he carried a giant pipe wrench that must have been three feet long.

"Can't you read? This is private property!"

Melissa, who didn't like confrontation, stepped behind Griffin and tried to make herself small.

Griffin spoke up. "It's our shortcut to school. Mrs. Martindale says it's okay."

The man stepped closer. His eyes seemed to burn even wilder. "Mrs. Martindale doesn't live here anymore. I do. And I don't allow strangers on my lawn."

"We're not strangers," Griffin explained. "We all live around here. Uh—welcome to the neighborhood." He manufactured a grin.

The newcomer's burning look grew no friendlier. "I like my privacy. As a matter of fact, I insist on it. And I don't care how Mrs. Martindale used to do things."

"But how are we supposed to get to school?" Ben asked plaintively.

The pipe wrench must have been growing heavy, because the man hefted it. "It's not my business whether or not you go to school, just so long as you stay off my property."

"The thing is," Pitch tried to reason, "without the cut-through, we have to go all the way up to Ninth Street. It takes at least an extra fifteen minutes. Maybe twenty."

"Then I guess you'd better get right on it."

He stood there and watched as they trudged away. As they passed the front walk, Griffin read the newly stickered name on the signpost.

"Ezekiel Hartman," he said bitterly.

"Hah!" snorted Ben. "Ezekiel *Heartless* would be more like it!"

They were only halfway to school when they heard the bell ring.

Griffin was furious. "The nerve of that guy! Who does he think he is?"

"He *thinks* he's the owner of that house," Pitch returned. "And he is."

"Mrs. Martindale's been talking about retiring to Florida for a long time," Melissa put in, puffing a little from walking so fast. "I guess she finally did it."

"He threatened us with a giant wrench!" Griffin raged. "That's a deadly weapon."

"No, he didn't," Ben argued. "He was probably fixing something when he saw us, so he had it in his hands when he came outside. He may be a big jerk, but he isn't a murderer."

"Kids have been cutting through there forever," Griffin said resentfully. "How long has he been here? A weekend? And now he thinks he can change all the rules! Well, we don't have to put up with it! We need a—"

"No!" Ben cut him off. "Not the *P* word! Not again! My mother says the next time you talk about a plan, I have to run in the opposite direction."

"She also wants you to get good grades," Griffin reasoned. "And how are you supposed to do that when you're late for school every day?"

"I have a plan," Melissa ventured timidly. "We wake up earlier so there's plenty of time to walk to school the long way."

Griffin stared at her. "You're kidding, right? That's not a plan; that's giving in."

"I can't get in trouble," Logan said firmly. "I've landed a major part in a TV commercial. It's a pivotal moment in my acting career, so nothing can interfere with my concentration while I'm getting into the role."

"Okay," Griffin agreed, "but think about the rehearsal time you'll be missing during all that extra walking."

Pitch was disgusted. "You guys are such airheads. We'll go the long way for a couple of weeks until

Heartless stops looking for us. Then we start sneaking through the shortcut again. Problem solved, plan-free."

At the school, the late bell rang. "Come on, let's run!"

And Griffin did, jogging alongside his friends. But deep down, he sensed there were problems ahead.

The kind of problems that couldn't be solved without the *P* word.

They got to school just as Savannah was being dropped off by her mother.

"How's Luthor?" Ben asked. He always inquired about Luthor because he was scared to death of the big Doberman. To some degree, they all were. Savannah's "Sweetie" had mellowed, but it never took much to turn him back into the ferocious guard dog he'd once been.

Savannah had tears in her eyes. "He's grounded," she said tragically. "It kills me to do it, but it's for his own safety. Every year, thousands of dogs are injured or worse because they chase cars."

"What does *grounded* mean for a dog?" asked Pitch. "No TV?"

"He has to stay tied up, and no playing with Cleopatra." Cleopatra was Savannah's pet capuchin monkey, and Luthor's best friend.

"That's harsh," Griffin said absently.

They checked in at the office for late passes and headed for their lockers. As they navigated the hallway, the doors to the auditorium were flung wide open, and students began to pour out.

"Aw, man, we missed an assembly!" Pitch complained. "I wonder if they said anything about the wrestling team."

"You mean besides the fact that you're not on it?" Logan inquired innocently.

She glared at him. "Go rehearse for your commercial. What is it this time? Another miracle cure for foot odor?"

Logan was insulted. "If you must know, it's for the Ouch-Free Bandage Company."

In the passing parade of students, a seventh-grade girl beamed at Griffin. "Hey, congratulations!"

"Thanks," replied Griffin, frowning a little. "Uh — what for?"

But she had already disappeared down the busy corridor.

It happened again. An eighth-grade boy slapped Griffin on the shoulder. "Way to go, man. You're a cinch," he announced before melting into the crowd.

Griffin looked at Ben. "Have I done anything lately?"

Ben just shrugged.

Nothing else was said, but Griffin could feel a lot of eyes on him as he made his way to math class that morning.

Mr. Kropotkin applauded as Griffin and Ben took their seats. "There he is—the man of the hour!" the teacher announced. "We're expecting great things from you, Griffin."

"What's going on?" Griffin asked finally. "Why is everybody congratulating me?"

"Weren't you at the assembly?" the teacher demanded. "Dr. Egan announced that our school will be competing in the Invent-a-Palooza this year."

Ben was mystified. "Invent-a-pa-*what*?"

"It's a national contest to find the best young inventors under the age of fifteen," Mr. Kropotkin explained. "With your background, Griffin, we're expecting you to put Cedarville on the map."

"My *background*?" Griffin repeated. Then he realized what everyone else must have been thinking: Griffin's father was a professional inventor with several patents under his belt, including one for the SmartPick™, a high-tech fruit-harvesting device.

"Hey, yeah!" Ben exclaimed. "Maybe you inherited some of your dad's inventor genes. I bet you could come up with something just as good as his stuff. Only, you know, not quite so fruity."

Oh, how Griffin hoped not! He was proud of his father's success, but he had always been a little embarrassed by the inventions themselves—telescoping fruit-picking poles, bushel-basket scooters, vole traps, and robotic pesticide sprayers, to name a few. Who needed all that fancy stuff to pick a few apples? Plus, it wasn't as if Mr. Bing were raking in millions from his creations. It was hard to make a living as a professional inventor.

"I don't know," Griffin said uncomfortably. "Maybe I won't enter. Just because my dad invents stuff doesn't mean I'm going to be good at it."

At that moment, big Darren Vader barreled into the room, his mouth flapping as always. At the sight of Griffin, he pretended to be overwhelmed, backing into Ben's desk and knocking it over, strewing books and papers onto the floor.

"Am I in the presence of Invent-a-Palooza royalty?" Darren gasped.

"Can it, Vader," Griffin groaned.

"He's so modest!" the burly boy crowed. "If my dad was a genius like yours, who knows what I could invent? Maybe even the wheel!"

"I think that's been invented already, Darren," said Mr. Kropotkin in annoyance.

"You can stop making such a big deal out of it," Griffin said through clenched teeth. "I'm not entering."

Darren staggered in feigned shock, stepping on Ben's fingers as the smaller boy stooped to pick up his scattered assignments.

"Ow!"

An agitated Ferret Face emerged from Ben's sleeve to investigate the cause of the disturbance.

"A Bing not entering?!" Darren exclaimed. "That's like Hercules wimping out on an arm-wrestling match!"

"Like you could do better!" Ben seethed, cradling his squashed fingers.

Darren beamed. "Funny you should mention it. I got so inspired during the assembly that I came up with an idea for an invention on the spot."

"Yeah? What?" Griffin challenged.

"Shame on you," Darren scolded. "You, of all people, must understand that a great inventor never gives up his secrets. Oops, I forgot—you don't know any *great* inventors."

"That's enough," said Mr. Kropotkin firmly. "Darren, take your seat."

"Or maybe invent one strong enough to carry the weight of your butt," Griffin murmured.

"Big talk from someone who's not even entering," Darren sneered.

"Oh, I'm entering, all right!" Griffin snapped. "Just to show you how it's done."

For the rest of the day, Griffin marched around the school, mentally kicking himself. How could he have allowed Darren to goad him into entering the contest? He didn't want to be an inventor! He didn't even really want his father to be an inventor! Sometimes he cursed the day the family had gone apple picking, and Mr. Bing had spoken those fateful words: *You know, there's got to be an easier way of doing this.*

He barely heard a word from his teachers, and even his friends couldn't get through to him. What if Darren had just been pulling his chain to trick him into signing up for a lot of extra work? There was no way Darren could be an inventor. The guy wasn't capable of creating anything more high-tech than intestinal gas, which he spread around pretty freely!

Or was he more of a threat than he seemed? Vader was no genius, but if there was anyone greedy enough to covet the prize money and fame of winning a national contest, it was him. Maybe he *did* have a good idea.

I have to find out for sure, Griffin decided. He raced through the halls, dodging students and weaving between rolling carts, coming to a breathless halt at the big bulletin board outside the office.

INVENT-A-PALOOZA — SIGN-UP SHEET

Scribbled on the first line, in what looked like purple crayon, was:

DARREN VADER

"I guess he wasn't bluffing, huh?"

Griffin jumped. He hadn't noticed Ben creeping up beside him. Before his friend could protest, Griffin pulled a pen out of his pocket and wrote his own name on line two.

"So what's your idea?" Ben asked.

Griffin shrugged. "Maybe my dad has some old

piece of junk I can pass off as my entry. If I let Vader beat me, I can never show my face in this town again."

"That's the spirit," Ben encouraged. "Let's bounce. We've got a long walk now that we can't use the shortcut anymore."

"Forget that," Griffin growled.

Ben frowned. "But Mr. Heartless said—"

"Heartless can keep us *out* of the shortcut because we have to cross his lawn to get there," Griffin explained. "But going the other way, we'll be across his property before he even sees us coming."

Ben was uncertain. "I don't want to fight with that guy. He looks kind of—odd."

"Who's fighting? We're just standing up for our rights."

They returned to their lockers, loaded up their book bags, and started for home. They were less than halfway through the shortcut when they could see that something up ahead was very different. Gone was the sawhorse with the NO TRESPASSING sign. In its place was a five-foot-high temporary wire fence. As they reached the edge of the trees, they noted that it stretched clear across the triangular strip of property, closing off all access to Honeybee Street.

Mr. Hartman stood in the center of the yard, leaning on a long-handled sledgehammer, glaring at them.

Cleopatra was raiding the pantry.

As Savannah hunched over the computer the next morning, scouring the Internet for hints on how to cure a dog of the dangerous habit of chasing cars, her pet monkey brought an endless supply of dog biscuits and milk bones to Luthor, who was tied to a stake in the front yard.

The leash was not what the Doberman was used to. In the Drysdale house, animals were treated as full family members. The menagerie included two cats, an ever-changing number of rabbits, hamsters, and guinea pigs, a pack rat, and an albino chameleon.

Luthor devoured the snacks, pathetically grateful to Cleopatra, who seemed to be the only friend who wasn't mad at him. Savannah was always yelling at him these days, although he couldn't imagine why.

A backfire sounded, and his ears perked up like the targeting system of a fighter jet locking on to an enemy plane. A moment later, there it was: the exterminator's red truck, passing right in front of the Drysdale house. He had to catch up to it. To his canine brain, nothing had ever been more urgent and necessary.

By the time he reached the end of the leash, Luthor was flying. The stake came out of the ground like a cork popping. He cleared the front hedge with at least a foot to spare, dragging the leash and the stake behind him. Then he was streaking down the street after his quarry, buoyed by a clear sense of purpose, and a hundred and fifty pounds of canine muscle and bone.

It was always the same. The great bearded face of Ralph the exterminator flashed in the side mirror, his eyes widened in shock and fear as the truck sped up along Honeybee Street.

It only made Luthor run harder.

"Thanks for the ride, Dad," Griffin told his father. "It takes forever to get to school now that Mr. Heartless fenced off our shortcut."

Mr. Bing eased to a halt at a stop sign. "Don't get used to it, kid. You're going to have to wake up earlier and leave yourself some extra time to walk to school. It's not rocket science. It can be done."

"It's so unfair!" Griffin groaned. "We weren't hurting anything, or making a mess, or even being loud. We were just cutting across the tip of his property."

"And those are the two magic words—*his property*. He can put a fence on it if he wants to."

Griffin made a face. "I'm going to be able to wall-paper my room with my late slips. Couldn't you just drive me until he moves away, or dies, or something?"

"I told you before, Griffin," his father explained patiently, "just because I work at home doesn't mean I'm not working. I know it seems like I'm tinkering around in the garage, but creating something that doesn't already exist is really hard."

I hope not, Griffin thought, the Invent-a-Palooza on his mind.

"So I'm happy to help you out when you're really in a bind," his father continued, making the turn onto Honeybee, "but I really don't have the time—"

The station wagon wheeled around the corner to come front grill to front grill with the exterminator's red truck. For a terrifying beat, the mouse hood orna-ment was right in their faces through the windshield. Then, at the last second, Ralph swerved to the right, driving up on the sidewalk. The two vehicles missed a sideswiping collision by mere inches.

Griffin exhaled. "That was clo—"

His relief lasted maybe one second. The instant the red truck swerved out of their path, it revealed a sec-ond incoming object, smaller but no less frightening. Luthor was hot on the tail of the exterminator, bound-ing headlong and heedless.

Mr. Bing slammed on the brakes, and so did Luthor. For a split second, a collision seemed inevitable. And then the two stopped dead, car and dog, a fraction of an inch apart.

Griffin leaped out of the car. "Luthor, are you hurt?"

The Doberman turned tail and trotted home at a leisurely pace, dragging his leash and the stake behind him.

Savannah came running out of the Drysdale house. Even at this distance, Griffin could hear her shrill voice, scolding her wayward dog. If she had seen how narrowly her Sweetie had avoided a tragic accident, she would have broken down completely.

Mr. Bing was white-faced and shaking. "Starting tomorrow," he breathed, "you walk."

4

OPERATION INVENT-A-PALOOZA

Objective: To beat Darren Vader in the contest.
Competition Level: Very low.
Procedure:
Step 1. Come up with a groundbreaking idea that improves
life for millions of ordinary people.
Step 2. . . .

Griffin sat back on the long cafeteria bench. He'd never get to Step 2 if he couldn't think of something to invent. He was known around Cedarville as The Man With The Plan. There was nothing, he believed, that couldn't be accomplished with the right strategy.

But for Invent-a-Palooza, all the planning in the world couldn't replace a flash of creative inspiration.

"Okay," he said to Ben. "What should we invent?"

"We?" As Ben took a bite of his sandwich, a tiny piece of roast beef fell from his lips. Ferret Face leaned out and snapped it up. "I didn't see *my* name anywhere on that sign-up sheet."

"Fine. What am *I* going to invent with the help of my best friend? It doesn't have to be that great. It just has to be greater than whatever Vader comes up with."

Ben frowned. "What does your dad say? How does he come up with his ideas?"

"He says you look at the world and you find something that's harder than it needs to be. Then you find a way to make it easier or better. So what's something in your life that's hard?"

"You're asking the wrong person," Ben replied honestly. "It's hard to wake up in the morning. It's hard to get to school with no shortcut. It's hard to get ferret fur out of your belly button. It's hard to be best friends with The Man With The Plan."

Griffin rolled his eyes and turned to Logan. "How about you? What would make your life easier?"

In response, Logan emitted an agonized *"Yeow!"* that echoed off the cafeteria's rafters.

Heads jerked in their direction. A lunch lady came running from the food line. "Are you all right?" she demanded, her hairnet askew.

Logan beamed proudly. "That wasn't screaming; it was *acting*. That cry of pain is from having a bandage removed that isn't Ouch-Free."

The lunch lady glowered at him. "Holler like that

again, buster, and *you* will not be ouch-free." She stormed back to her post.

Logan looked pleased, but thoughtful. "There must be some way to squeeze a little more suffering into my performance."

"For crying out loud," said Griffin, "they're removing a bandage, not cutting off your head!"

"The point is," Logan explained, "when they take off the Ouch-Free bandage, I don't cry out at—"

Suddenly, Logan burst forth with a *"Yeow!"* that was three times louder than the first one. He leaped to his feet and did a frantic dance. An ice cube dropped out of his shirt and hit the floor.

He wheeled to find Darren Vader standing over him, fingers still glistening with meltwater.

"What did you do that for?" Logan bawled.

Darren spread his arms in a gesture of innocence. "You try to help a guy rehearse, and this is the thanks you get. You were brilliant, man! I really believed you were hurting."

"All right, wise guy!" called the lunch lady from the food line. "You're gone!"

Logan turned furious eyes on Darren. "You got me kicked out of the cafeteria!"

"Way to suffer for your art, Kellerman. You can thank me later." Darren plopped his tray down in the spot Logan vacated. "How's the inventing coming along, Bing?" He gazed at Griffin's near-blank paper. "Diddly-squat. Real impressive."

"Like you're burning up the track," Griffin snorted, snatching his paper away.

Darren beamed. "As a matter of fact, my invention is well under way, and even you're going to have to admit that it's awesome."

"I'll admit that when you win," Griffin replied readily. "Or when pigs fly. Whichever comes first."

"I'll make you a deal," Darren proposed. "If I win the contest, you have to make a speech in front of the whole cafeteria about how great I am, and how you stink. And the speech will be written by me."

"Only if it works both ways," Griffin countered. "If I win, I get to write the speech for you. And trust me — when it comes to the subject of you stinking, I'm Shakespeare!"

The bell rang to signal the end of the period.

"Too bad, Vader," Griffin said in amusement. "Looks like you have no time to eat your lunch. I guess when you spend forty minutes loading your tray —"

In answer, Darren picked up his order of spaghetti and meatballs, squeezed the Styrofoam plate to form a chute, and dumped his entire lunch into his open mouth. He was still chewing and swallowing as they made their way through the halls, half his face stained with sauce.

"The garbage disposal has already been invented," Griffin informed him.

Darren awarded him an appreciative belch. "Nice one, Bing. You're still going to lose, but it was a good joke."

Ben sidled up to his best friend. "I hope you know

what you're doing, Griffin. If you have to stand in front of the whole school and say nice things about Vader, it's going to break your spirit."

"It'll never happen," Griffin promised.

"To *me*," Darren added.

"Maybe neither of you will win," said Ben. "There are a lot of middle schools in Nassau County."

Darren was confident. "I guarantee that nobody out there has what it takes to beat *my* idea."

"Except me," Griffin put in.

As they passed the main office and the bulletin board, the Invent-a-Palooza sign-up sheet came into view. They all saw it at the same time—there was a third name added to the list under Darren and Griffin.

"Hey!" exclaimed Darren. "Who's horning in on our contest?"

They approached the bulletin board. The third name was written in pencil, and so faintly that it was difficult to make out from a distance. But when they got closer, they could read the neat, precise signature perfectly.

Melissa Dukakis

5

M elissa?" Griffin was shocked and a little dismayed. Once he had his Invent-a-Palooza idea, he'd been planning to ask for Melissa's help with it. She was a bona fide computer and tech wizard with mad skills Darren could never even dream of.

Now not only was Griffin losing those skills, but they would be out there working against him *and* Darren.

"Uh-oh," said Ben. "It looks like both you guys are going to be making speeches about Melissa."

Darren brayed a laugh in Griffin's face. "Tough break. Looks like your chief nerd is going into business for herself."

Griffin opened his mouth to defend Melissa, but for some reason, the words did not come — not even as a retort to Darren, which should have been automatic. The fact that she was entering this contest against him felt almost like a slap in the face. She had been a member of his team since the very beginning. It wasn't so much that she had no right to enter, but why did she even want to? And why wouldn't she warn him first?

"Come on, Ben," Griffin said. They abandoned Darren, who was still licking spaghetti sauce from the corners of his mouth.

"Where are we going?" Ben asked. "Social studies is *that* way."

"We're not going to social studies," Griffin said grimly. "We're going to talk to Melissa."

Ben slowed down. "Wait a minute. You're not going to give her a hard time about this, are you? It'll freak her out. You know how shy she is."

"She wasn't very shy when she put her name up on that sign-up sheet," Griffin reminded him.

"Yeah, okay, that was kind of a surprise," Ben admitted. "Still—free country, right?"

But Griffin was already wheeling around the corner to the hall where Melissa had her locker. There she was, stowing books and sneaking a glance at the messages on one of the handheld devices she'd custom made for herself.

The curtain of hair parted and one eye peered out. "Hi, Griffin."

"Melissa, what were you thinking, signing up for the Invent-a-Palooza?"

The girl looked worried. "I thought it would be fun."

"It *could* be fun," Griffin agreed, "if you were on my team, like you always are."

At that moment, Pitch came around the corner, breathing fire. "Well, it's over. The word just came in from Coach. No wrestling." She noticed the distressed expression on Melissa's face. "What did I miss?"

Ben jumped into the silence. "Griffin's a little bent out of shape over the contest."

"I'm not bent out of shape," Griffin amended. "It's just that, well, we normally do things as a team—"

"It's okay," Melissa said quickly. "I'll take my name off the list. I'll quit."

"Hold up." Pitch turned to Griffin. "How is it your business if Melissa wants to enter?"

"It isn't," Griffin admitted lamely, "except that I was kind of counting on her help with *my* entry."

Pitch's eyes narrowed. "Oh, I get it. Because *your* entry matters, and hers doesn't. And why is that? Because you're a *guy*, maybe?"

Griffin stared at her. "What's that got to do with anything?"

Pitch was bitter. "It's easy for you to pretend these things aren't important. Nobody ever told you that you can't wrestle, or suggested maybe you should go out for cheerleading."

Now Ben was confused. "Who said anything about cheerleading?"

"When you're born male," Pitch explained resentfully, "no one ever lectures you on what you can't do. Like running for president. Or wrestling. Or being an inventor. Let me tell you something: Melissa is going to invent something so amazing it'll leave you and Vader in the dust!"

Melissa looked haunted behind her curtain of hair. "I really don't want to make trouble. . . ."

"That's another thing girls aren't supposed to do," Pitch snarled. "Don't rock the boat. Don't make a fuss. Keep the peace. That ends today. Anything boys can invent, girls can invent better. Come on, Melissa. Let's get out of here and start working on your idea."

Melissa shut her locker, and Pitch dragged her off, gesturing animatedly with both hands.

Ben watched them go, stunned. "What just happened?"

"So much for getting any help from Melissa."

"That's all you got out of that?" Ben exploded. "Two of our best friends just accused us of discrimination!"

"And they lumped me together with Vader," Griffin added in an annoyed tone. "Just because we're both boys! You want to talk discrimination—how about that?"

Ben thought it over. "And I'm a guy, so that includes me. I'm nothing like Vader! When did *I* ever drink a whole plate of spaghetti and meatballs?"

Griffin was disgusted. "Not only am I up against Vader, I'm up against Melissa, too."

"She'll be tough to beat," said Ben. "She's a total genius."

Griffin nodded soberly. "She's already forgotten

more about technology than we're ever going to know. Now I *really* need a plan."

Daylight was fading, but Melissa did not turn on the lights in her bedroom. She sat amid the blinking indicators on the various computers, printers, modems, routers, signal boosters, tablets, webcams, and handheld devices that stood and sat all around the room. It was a comfortable place for her to be, bathed in the dim glow of screens, immersed in the underlying hum of all these electronics.

Equipment was easy to understand. It did what it was programmed to do. Its quirks could be debugged, its short circuits repaired. It was not nearly so easy to understand people.

Melissa had never had any friends before Griffin had recruited her for his team. She had been with Griffin, Ben, Savannah, Pitch, and Logan through all their operations and adventures. And now it was all in jeopardy. Griffin was mad at her for entering, and Pitch would be mad at her if she backed out. She was caught between a rock and a hard place, with a very real chance of losing the friends she had come to treasure.

And the worst part of all was that she didn't even have an idea for an invention. She could make a computer do whatever she wanted it to; she could think in programming code; she understood robotics; she could design and build complicated electronics, hydraulics, and pneumatics. In short, if you told her what to do, she could do it better than anybody.

But that original idea, the spark, just wasn't there.

What could she invent? She kept telling herself that there must be some need she could fill, some problem she could solve. It had to be so obviously worthwhile that Griffin and Pitch would stop bickering and start supporting her on it.

But what? There were plenty of problems in the world, but nothing she could solve with a gadget, even a brilliant one.

A commotion outside drew her attention to the window. The exterminator's red truck weaved down the block at an unsafe speed, its driver obviously in a great hurry. Only a few feet behind it, a black-and-tan blur raced along, trying to catch up. Behind that ran Savannah, waving her arms. The window was shut, so the scene had no audio. But it had been played out so many times before that Melissa could imagine the sound track: the backfire of the engine, Luthor's barking, and Savannah's voice calling, "Luthor! Sweetie! Come back!"

She felt bad for her friend. Savannah had so much animal knowledge, yet it didn't seem to be working on the one animal who meant the most to her. That had to be as frustrating as Melissa not being able to quarantine a simple computer virus. But this was worse, because a broken computer could be replaced. If Luthor was hurt or killed because of his dangerous behavior, Savannah would never get over it.

An unfamiliar feeling came over Melissa. It was not her usual talent for breaking complex challenges down into simple algorithms.

No, this was pure inspiration.

Suddenly, she knew exactly what her Invent-a-Palooza project was going to be.

6

For the last time, Griffin, I won't do your project for you. It wouldn't be fair. And besides, I've got my own inventions to worry about."

Griffin stood in the doorway of his father's small study. Mr. Bing was at his desk, surrounded by cartons that served as file cabinets. He was crouched in front of a computer screen, filling in an online patent form using a single hunt-and-peck index finger.

"Come on, Dad," Griffin said in his most wheedling tone. "It's your fault I'm in this mess to begin with."

"*My* fault?" His father swiveled around in his chair. "How do you figure that?"

"I'm the inventor's son. The minute the school decided to be a part of the Invent-a-Palooza, all eyes were on me. Even the teachers are expecting me to put Cedarville on the map. How am I supposed to do that if you won't even help?"

"I never said I wouldn't help," his father explained patiently. "But the idea has to come from you. Now please stop distracting me. You know how this paper-work goes. If you get a single comma out of place, your whole application is rejected."

"Sorry, Dad." Before he could leave the office, an enormous wail went up in the house, and Mrs. Bing appeared at the end of the hall, vacuuming the rug.

Mr. Bing held his head. "So much for working!"

Griffin nodded in agreement. "Too bad there's no such thing as a silent vacuum."

"Silent?" his father repeated. "I'd settle for being able to hear myself scream. B-52s are quieter than that thing." He frowned, and looked up to face his son. "Why don't you invent one?"

"Invent what? A vacuum cleaner? Somebody already did."

"A *quiet* vacuum cleaner," his father amended. "One that doesn't sound as if the whole house is about to take off at the airport."

"I don't know anything about vacuum cleaners," Griffin protested.

"You don't have to," his father insisted. "Most of the operating noise comes from the motor. If you could design a quiet, well-muffled motor for small and medium-sized appliances, that would be an excellent invention."

The vacuum cleaner noise swelled as Mrs. Bing roared past the study.

Mr. Bing shouted over it. "And as the owner of two perforated eardrums, I promise to help."

"Thanks, Dad. That's great!" For the first time since the Invent-a-Palooza had been sprung on him, Griffin began to toy with the idea that there might actually be a way out of this mess. He wasn't totally convinced that a quiet motor was such a big deal. But it had to be better than anything Vader could come up with.

Griffin was the only one who heard the doorbell over the roar of the vacuum. When he answered it, Logan stood on the front stoop, an annoyed expression on his face.

"The girls won't pinch me!"

Griffin stared at him. "Uh—why do you want them to?"

"It's called method acting. You have to *live* your role. When I say 'ouch' in that commercial, it has to come from true experience. Melissa promised to help me prepare, but when I got to her house, Savannah and Pitch were both there. They told me she's too busy and kicked me out."

Griffin sighed. "It's a long story. Pitch is all gung ho about Melissa's Invent-a-Palooza entry because the school wouldn't put her on the wrestling team. She's turning it into a whole girls-versus-boys thing."

Logan looked worried. "Oh. That explains why they got so mad. I kind of messed up a little."

"What did you do?"

"I told them I was the 'leading man' of the commercial. And then"—he flushed—"I tried to explain the history of the leading man in Hollywood—how, over the years, top actors have brought in more box office than actresses. It got ugly. Pitch said she couldn't pinch me, but how would I like it if she knocked my teeth down my throat? Then Savannah slammed the door in my face. I never saw Melissa at all."

"You're lucky," Griffin assured him. "She compared Ben and me to Vader. Talk about a low blow."

Logan stuck around that afternoon, and Ben came over later. They spent the day taking apart the Bings' old vacuum cleaner. They removed the motor and broke it down into its component parts to see exactly how it operated. It was surprisingly simple — a central rotor with a stationary cylinder around it. Both parts featured a lot of tightly coiled wire, which — according to Wikipedia — created the electromagnetic force that caused the rotor to spin.

"Right," said Ben. "I'm ready to call Melissa now. How about you guys?"

"Never!" Griffin snapped. "That's just what they're counting on us to do. I'll bet Pitch is waiting for me to phone so she can use it as proof that boys aren't as smart as girls. Well, she'll wait a long time."

Next they reassembled the motor, which went smoothly, except that there were a couple of parts left over. Stage three was to put it back into the vacuum cleaner. It worked perfectly except for one detail: The machine now blew out instead of sucking in. An enormous cloud of black dirt filled Griffin's room, leaving the three boys choking.

Ferret Face abandoned Ben's shirt and tried to crawl under the door. He got stuck halfway through and lay there squealing.

Mrs. Bing yelled a lot, and would probably still be yelling if her husband hadn't intervened.

"Come on, now," Mr. Bing said. "You can't be married to me all these years and not know that the inventing process has much more failure than success."

"Yeah, but when a SmartPick fails, you get a squashed apple, not a mountain of soot three feet high!"

So Mr. Bing made room for them in his workshop in the garage. He even helped them reassemble the motor properly.

"Okay," said Logan. "Showtime." He reached for the switch.

"Not yet!" bellowed Mr. Bing in a panic.

Too late. The instant Logan's finger touched the power button, a spark as bright as forked lightning lit up the garage.

"Yeow!"

He was thrown back against a shelving unit, scattering ratchet heads far and wide. He sank to the concrete floor, dazed, a tuft of dark smoke issuing from the crown of his head.

Mr. Bing, Griffin, and Ben leaped to his rescue.

Mr. Bing slapped his cheeks. "Logan! Can you hear me? Are you all right?"

"That's it!" Logan croaked, his face blissful.

Griffin's father was shaken. "Do you need to go to the hospital?"

"Not the hospital! A soundstage!"

Mr. Bing's alarm was growing. "He's not making any sense!"

"Calm down, Dad," Griffin soothed. "That's just Logan. He's finally found the perfect yell for his latest acting assignment."

"What's the part—Tarzan?"

At that moment, what was left of the vacuum cleaner burst into flames, and Mr. Bing covered it with fire extinguisher foam.

From then on, the motor was a lot quieter. It never worked again.

7

As the days leading up to the Invent-a-Palooza wore
on, what had once been a team of six friends
broke into two teams — one of three boys and one of
three girls. Nowhere was this more obvious than at the
school cafeteria. The boys ate lunch at a table just
beyond the food line. The girls chose a spot in a distant corner of the room, as far away from the boys as
possible. There was zero communication between the
two factions, except for Melissa's occasional unhappy
look across the space. And since she was usually clois-
tered behind her hair, no one really noticed that.
Mostly, the groups did their best to appear happy and
unconcerned, as though the current situation was just
fine with them, thank you very much. And if that attitude was a little less than the truth, neither side was
willing to admit it.

A piece of paper was interposed between Griffin
and his sandwich. He looked up questioningly to find
Darren Vader flopping onto the bench beside him.

"It's just a first draft," the big boy apologized, "but I'd love to get your opinion."

Griffin glanced at the page, which was scribbled in a handwriting that would not have been out of place in a third-grade classroom.

MY FELLOW CEDARVILLAINS,

I STAND BEFORE YOU, THE LOWEST OF THE LOW, FAR LOWER THAN THE SLIME TRAIL OF A GARBAGE-EATING SLUG, TO CONGRATULATE THE GREAT DARREN VADER FOR DESTROYING ME IN THE INVENT-A-PALOOZA, EVEN THOUGH I AM SO BRAINLESS AND UNTALENTED THAT BEATING ME IS SOMETHING ANY BABY BABOON COULD DO WITH HIS BANANA-PEELING HAND TIED BEHIND HIS BACK . . .

"How do you like it so far?" Darren asked sweetly.

"The word is *Cedarvillian*, not *Cedarvillain*," Griffin managed through a fiery haze.

"Keep reading," Darren urged. "You haven't gotten to the good part yet."

Griffin skipped to the bottom.

. . . AND SO I APOLOGIZE TO DARREN, FOR DARING TO BELIEVE I HAVE AS MUCH BRAINS IN MY ENTIRE BODY AS HE HAS IN HIS PINKY TOENAIL; TO MY PARENTS, FOR BEING SUCH A HORRIBLE DISAPPOINTMENT; AND TO THE WORLD, FOR TAKING UP SPACE THAT COULD BE USED FOR SOMEONE WORTHWHILE.

FINALLY, I APOLOGIZE TO YOU, MY FELLOW
CEDARVILLAINS, FOR USING SUCH SMALL WORDS. I
AM EXTREMELY STUPID, AND LARGER WORDS BOUNCE
AROUND MY EMPTY HEAD AND SOMETIMES MISS MY
MOUTH. NOW PLEASE EXCUSE ME. MY DROOL BUCKET
NEEDS TO BE EMPTIED. . . .

The hardest part for Griffin was that Ben laughed out loud. He'd been smirking a little, but the drool bucket put him over the top.

"What *is* this?" Griffin demanded to Darren.

"Your speech," Darren replied. "Don't tell me you're trying to weasel out of our deal. No offense," he added in an aside to Ferret Face. "The winner gets to write the loser's speech."

"You haven't won anything yet," Griffin noted darkly.

"Excuse me for being confident." Darren beamed. "My invention is running way ahead of schedule, and your tech consultant . . ." He squinted across the cafeteria to where Melissa sat with the other girls. "Is that still the United States over there? I always forget where Canada starts."

"Well, my invention is coming along great, too," Griffin boasted.

"It was a turning point in my acting career," added Logan proudly. "The electric shock I got when the vacuum cleaner blew up—" He fell silent as Ben kicked him under the table.

"Sounds like you're doing awesome, Bing," Darren commented. "Tell you what—I'll also throw in a speech for Kellerman for when he gets his Academy Award. No extra charge." He stood up. "Oh, wow, they refilled the tater tots. I'll get a big plate for the table. You can't memorize your speech on an empty stomach."

"What are you going to do, Griffin?" Ben whispered once Darren was gone. "You've got no invention. Your only hope is that Melissa schools all of us."

"That's even worse," Griffin said stubbornly. "Speech or no, the girls would really rub our faces in it."

"You're running out of vacuum cleaners," Logan warned.

"There's an even older one in the basement. And Dad's promised to help me with the wiring this time." Griffin's eyes shot sparks. "I'd like to see Melissa and the girls come up with something to compete with that!"

8

Ha!" Pitch was triumphant. "I'd like to see Griffin and the boys come up with something to compete with this!"

The girls were gathered at the Drysdale home for the official unveiling of Melissa's invention. They gazed down at the device in the wagon. It looked like a silver TV cable box, topped with an X-shaped superstructure. At the four tips of the X were miniature rotor blades.

"I call it the Hover Handler," Melissa said modestly.

"It's amazing!" Savannah breathed, her eyes wide. "But how is it going to stop Luthor from chasing cars?"

"I've added a GPS chip to Luthor's collar," Melissa explained, her curtain of hair parting with the enthusiasm of the telling. "When the system detects him running into the road, the Hover Handler will deploy and stop him before he can put himself in danger."

Savannah was worried. "It won't hurt him, will it?"

"It won't touch him at all," Melissa promised. "The unit emits a sound so high-pitched that humans can barely hear it. But it should be irritating enough to Luthor to keep him from running into traffic."

"How do we test it?" asked Pitch, all business.

"All you have to do is lead him out into the street," Melissa explained. "Once the GPS transmitter's in the road, it will signal the Hover Handler to come and get him."

Savannah shook her head. "What kind of message would that send? If he obeys me and something unpleasant happens, I'd be stabbing him in the back. I'd lose all credibility."

Pitch was growing impatient. "You don't need credibility with a dog. All you need is hamburger."

Savannah was wounded. "How can you say that, knowing what a sensitive, intelligent creature Luthor is?"

Melissa looked worried. "But we can't wait around all day for the exterminator's truck to go by. That's not a practical way to run your test."

Savannah was stubborn. "I refuse to betray his trust."

Pitch took a paper bag from the wagon and dumped out a few spare batteries. She squeezed the opening of the bag, brought it to her lips, and puffed it full of air. "The truck backfires, right?" And with a flourish, she slammed her palm into the bag.

POP!!

In the side yard, Luthor's cropped ears stood straight up. His canine brain instantly connected the dots. In this neighborhood, only one thing made a noise like that. *It* was coming! And this time he was going to catch it!

He bounded over the hedge and catapulted off the sidewalk, craning his neck in an attempt to spot the oncoming red truck. The instant his leaping body passed over the curb, the four miniature rotor blades on the Hover Handler began to spin at high speed. The metallic unit lifted off the wagon and shot straight up in the air, acquiring the signal of the transmitter on Luthor's collar. A split second later, it was locked on. It dropped back down and came to float over the big Doberman. A faint, high-pitched ringing sounded out over the entire neighborhood. It was barely audible to the girls, but the effect on Luthor was nothing short of amazing. He broke out of his run, lifted up onto his hind legs, and began what looked like a strange, leaping hip-hop dance, front paws pumping rhythmically.

The girls stared, open-mouthed. Even Melissa, who had designed the device, was overwhelmed by its ability to control a hundred and fifty pounds of raw canine power.

Savannah thought she knew everything there was to know about her beloved pet, but this was something she never could have imagined.

Pitch watched as Luthor sashayed over to the sidewalk and hopped up to safety. "Now there's something you don't see too often."

The instant Luthor was no longer in the road, the

Hover Handler returned to its base in the wagon and shut itself off.

Luthor licked Savannah's hand absently. Whatever it was that had so galvanized his attention a moment before, he couldn't remember it at all now.

Savannah regarded the Hover Handler's inventor with even more respect than before. "If this cures Luthor of chasing that truck, I will never be able to thank you enough!" she exclaimed emotionally. "You might have just saved his life."

"Plus, we're going to wreck those guys at Invent-a-Palooza," Pitch added with relish. "It's going to be a blowout. If there's a mercy rule for paloozas, they're going to have to invoke it!"

"I never could have done it without GPS technology," Melissa said modestly. Praise made her feel uncomfortable. She turned away from her friends and, through the dangling strands of hair, caught sight of a familiar figure marching purposefully in their direction, his face a thundercloud. "Isn't that Mr. Hartman?"

"I've never seen him leave his property before," Savannah remarked. "He sure is steamed about something."

All three looked around, trying to spot the source of the new neighbor's anger. When he came to a halt, it was directly in front of them.

"Don't think I can't see what you're doing! You're spying on me!"

"Spying?" echoed Pitch. "How?"

Mr. Hartman pointed to the Hover Handler sitting on its base in the wagon. "With that thing! I saw it up in the air, taking pictures of my house!"

"No!" The sheer unfairness of the accusation caused Melissa to find her voice. "It's not for spying — it's a Hover Handler!" In a halting voice, the shy girl blurted out a disjointed explanation of exactly what the device did, and why.

"In a world where everybody lies," he pronounced, "starting with the government clear on down to children on the street, that is the most ridiculous tall tale I've ever been told! What kind of person is gullible enough to believe in an invention as cockamamie as a Hover Handler?"

There was the roar of an old engine, punctuated by a small backfire, and the red truck from Ralph's Exterminators turned onto Honeybee and started up the incline. A split second later, Luthor's huge front paws were on Mr. Hartman's shoulders as he launched himself over the terrified man and hit the road running. Mr. Hartman had barely recovered from that shock when the Hover Handler lifted off its base and started after Luthor — on a direct collision course with the neighbor's flushed, angry face.

In a desperate move of self-preservation, Mr. Hartman dropped to the sidewalk in the duck-and-cover position. The Hover Handler hurtled skyward, passing through the space that had just been occupied by the unfriendly neighbor's head. The helicopter-like device dropped down over Luthor and emitted its high-pitched sound. Once again, the big Doberman gave up the chase and broke into his dance, grooving his way to the safety of the sidewalk.

"That," said Pitch in a for-your-information tone, "is a Hover Handler. Neat, huh?"

Mr. Hartman picked himself up and dusted off his clothes. "Keep that gadget away from me and my property. And that goes for your dog, too." He stormed off toward home.

The girls watched his retreating back.

Pitch caught her breath. "Wow. An invention that saves Luthor, puts the guys in their place, and has Heartless diving for his life. I think I'm in love."

9

Y ou know," Logan said, pleasantly surprised, "I think that's a little quieter than before."

"It's definitely quieter," Ben agreed. "Ferret Face is very sensitive to vibration, and he's a lot calmer now."

"We're a genius!" Griffin cheered, sashaying around as he vacuumed the basement rug.

Logan joined in, acting out an imaginary commercial. "Is your vacuum so loud that you can't hear the air-raid siren? Behold, the Invent-a-Palooza-winning new vacuum from Griffin Bing. Voice-over provided by Logan Kellerman, resume available on request."

A long, twitching needle nose protruded from Ben's sleeve.

"Guys, I think Ferret Face smells something."

Griffin sniffed. "Smoke!" he exclaimed. He put his hand on the motor housing and found it hot to the touch. He wrenched the plug out of the wall. Another fire would be catastrophic to his supply of test motors. The instant he opened up the vacuum, a gray cloud rose up and dispersed. The problem was instantly visible. The heavy fleece muffling material was singed black and smoldering. He picked it up gingerly between thumb and forefinger and tossed it in the laundry sink. "Ow!"

"That's a pretty impressive *ow*," Logan appraised. "Definitely not professional-actor quality, but with practice —"

"I burned my fingers!" Griffin howled.

"Don't tell me we've killed another vacuum cleaner," Ben groaned.

When the motor was cool enough to handle again, they wiped off the scorch with a damp cloth and reinserted it into the vacuum. The machine roared to life, undamaged — but, of course, loud as ever.

"What now?" asked Logan, discouraged. "We can't just keep stuffing it with old sweatshirt material. We'll burn your house down."

"My dad said this should work," Griffin explained. "We just have to find material that's thin enough that the motor can still breathe. But if the material's too thin, it won't muffle the sound. It might even burn more easily."

"Maybe you should talk to my mother," Ben suggested. "She reads all these parenting-magazine articles about dressing your kids in clothes made out of fire-retardant material."

Griffin perked up. "Fire-retardant material?"

Ben flushed. "I happen to be one of the only middle schoolers who has to wear fire-retardant pajamas."

"Well, why didn't you say so? Go get them!"

Ben made a face. "I don't want to."

"Why not?" Griffin demanded.

His friend was tight-lipped. "They're—inappropriate."

Logan spoke up. "Inappropriate how?"

"They've got bunny rabbits, okay?" Ben exploded. "It's not my fault! I'm short, so I still fit into a lot of little kid stuff."

Griffin was baffled. "How come I've never seen those?"

"Well, I don't wear them for sleepovers, you know," Ben shot back. "Sometimes it's better to risk going up in flames."

"Listen to me," Griffin said through clenched teeth. "Those girls are going to wipe the floor with us, and we'll never hear the end of it. Or worse, Vader might win. If I have to make that speech, your name is going to come up more than once. Now get those pajamas."

Fifteen minutes later, Griffin worked with a pair of scissors to cut a large circle out of the seat of a pair of bunny-rabbit pajamas. He wrapped the fabric carefully around the motor and reinserted it into the vacuum cleaner. "Here goes nothing."

He flicked the switch. The vacuum started again, quiet like before. So far, so good. They could feel suction coming from the base. The housing warmed up but didn't seem to be overheating.

Ben removed Ferret Face from his shirt and held the little creature right up to the vacuum. The needle nose didn't twitch, and he didn't seem agitated or perturbed.

"No smoke," Ben concluded.

"Keep it going," Griffin said intently. "We have no idea how long the Invent-a-Palooza judges will make us run it. If it burns out in the middle of the contest, I'm dead meat."

But after several minutes, the motor was still on an even keel, humming quietly, warm but not burning.

For the first time, Griffin dared to hope. "I think maybe we've got it."

"That's a wrap!" cheered Logan.

"You did it, man," Ben added in admiration. "Congratulations."

Mr. Bing was in his garage workshop when it happened. The lights went out, and the electric drill in his hand fell silent, spiraling to a halt halfway through a sheet of metal.

A power failure? He poked his head out of the

garage and checked on the neighbors' houses. Everybody had lights except the Bings.

A circuit breaker, then. He must have blown a fuse.

He entered the house, grabbed a flashlight, and ran down to the basement to check the electrical box. Everything seemed okay. Funny. That was when he noticed the hum coming from the playroom. It was a soft sound, yet definitely electrical.

But the power was out. What was going on around here?

He opened the playroom door, shone the beam inside, and stared in amazement. There stood his son, flanked by Ben and Logan. Griffin had a hold of the old vacuum cleaner. It was plugged in. And it was *working*! How could that be? You didn't have to be a professional inventor to understand that a house with no electricity can't run a vacuum cleaner!

"Griffin," Mr. Bing called. And then louder: *"Griffin!"*

Spying him, Griffin flicked the off switch on the vacuum. The hum of the motor died, and something else happened, something not even Mr. Bing could explain.

The clock on the cable box lit up. The refrigerator whirred to life. The computer rebooted. A radio began to play. And every light in the house came back on.

10

Gadgets had never been Savannah's thing. Animals were her passion, not technology. But she had to admit that she loved the Hover Handler beyond reason. No more did she lie awake at night tortured by images of her beloved Luthor lying injured, or worse, by the side of the road. It was changing her life.

Melissa had made a few minor adjustments. For example, she had waterproofed the unit, since Luthor could chase the exterminator's truck in rain or shine. The device was now deployed in the middle of the front lawn, connected to the house by an extension cord. The base doubled as a charging station, keeping the Hover Handler fully juiced and ready to go.

The one thing it didn't solve was the mystery of why Luthor was chasing Ralph's vehicle—and *only* Ralph's vehicle. But Savannah was enough of a dog expert to understand and accept that she might never know the answer. Animals had personalities with quirks and hang-ups, just like people. Luthor was a swirl of contradictions: his guard-dog training versus his sweet and gentle nature, memories of his awful former owner versus the loving home that was his now.

And anyway, whatever the cause of his problem, Melissa's fantastic invention had it under control. If the Hover Handler didn't win first prize at the Invent-a-Palooza, the judges were all idiots. She felt an uncomfortable stab of anger against Griffin, even though he had always been a loyal friend to her and Luthor. Where did Griffin get off treating Melissa like a junior partner just because she was a girl? And didn't it figure that Ben and Logan would throw their chips in with Griffin, since they were boys, too. Like there was any question that Melissa was the superior inventor, no matter who Griffin's dad happened to be!

Savannah wasn't the only one who appreciated how the Hover Handler had made life better. Yesterday, Ralph, the exterminator, had arrived at the Drysdales' door carrying a huge fruit basket.

"I don't know how you did it," the man had said emotionally, "but thanks! I've been having nightmares about what that dog would do to my truck if he ever caught up to it."

Savannah had smiled tolerantly. "He's really a big softie." She hefted the basket. "You didn't have to do this. It must have cost a lot of money."

A shrug. "That's okay, kid. It's a lot cheaper than moving my office to another town."

Not everyone was a fan of the new invention. The nearsighted Mrs. Calhoun, who lived two doors down, reported to the police that there was a large predatory bird chasing ponies in the neighborhood. And, of course, there was Mr. Hartman. Savannah had spotted the unwelcome, unfriendly neighbor standing by his fence, searching the sky with a camera equipped with a long telephoto lens. So far, no one on Honeybee Street had ever seen him smile.

Serves him right, Savannah reflected as she loaded up her backpack for the long roundabout walk to school early Monday morning. If it weren't for Mr. Heartless and his fence and his bad attitude, she would have had time for breakfast before this morning's meeting. Mr. Kropotkin wanted an update on the Invent-a-Palooza projects. Pitch insisted that all the girls be there to support Melissa, and to make sure their friend didn't get steamrolled by Griffin or stabbed in the back by Darren. It made a lot of sense. Melissa was a tech titan, but when it came to standing up for herself, she was a lamb.

Savannah was tying her sneakers when a telltale backfire sounded from out in the street. Next came Luthor's barking, and the percussive clomp of heavy footfalls as the big Doberman took off across the lawn in pursuit of the exterminator's truck. It was a tribute to Melissa's incredible invention that Savannah didn't even look up from her laces. She listened for the high-pitched tone of the Hover Handler. It never came. Instead, Luthor's barking continued, sounding ever more distant.

Forgetting everything else, including her second shoe, Savannah ran outside. A terrible sight met her eyes. Luthor was in full flight along the broken line at the center of Honeybee Street, in pursuit of the red truck with the mouse hood ornament. Just for an instant, she caught sight of Ralph's accusing face in the side mirror before he stomped on the gas and his vehicle leaped forward and out of sight. It may have been a trick of the light, but Savannah could have sworn that he mouthed the words *I want my fruit back!* before disappearing around the corner.

"Luthor! Come here this minute!" As she sprinted, one shoe off and one shoe on, after her dog, her mind was awhirl. What had happened? Why had the Hover Handler stopped working?

That was when she glanced behind her and saw it: a section of flattened grass in exactly the shape of the rechargeable base. The extension cord lay there, attached to nothing.

The Hover Handler was gone.

"My project," Griffin was telling Mr. Kropotkin, "is a quieter electric motor. You know how small appliances like blenders and vacuum cleaners are so noisy? Well, the SH-1 is designed to change all that."

"Excellent," the teacher approved, making a few notes on a ring-bound pad. "SH—does that stand for something?"

Griffin nodded. "It's short for *shhhh*."

"And is it completed?" probed Mr. Kropotkin.

"Yes," replied Griffin at the same time as Ben said, "No."

The teacher frowned, "Well, which is it?"

"Oh, it's totally ready," Griffin answered with a kick at Ben under the table. "There's just one minor detail that needs to be ironed out before we can bring it in. It doesn't affect the operation of the machine at all."

"A cosmetic issue," Mr. Kropotkin concluded.

"You might call it that," Griffin agreed.

Ben massaged his sore knee. Only Griffin could take what had happened with the SH-1 and call it *cosmetic*. The thing had shut off all the electricity in the Bing house. But it wasn't a loss of power—that at least would have made sense. There was plenty of power to run the SH-1. It was everything else that was stone-dead.

"The nearest I can explain it," a bewildered Mr. Bing had offered, "is that your motor sucked all the electricity out of the system and used it for itself."

And when a professional inventor says your project "defies the laws of science," most people would consider that a pretty big problem. Not The Man With The Plan, though.

When they'd opened up the motor, they'd discovered that the fabric of the bunny-rabbit pajamas had fused with the electromagnetic coils. Mr. Bing had suggested that some of the fire-retardant chemicals in the fabric might have reacted with the copper wiring. But he had no idea how or why. Even now, Griffin's father was poring over his old college science books in search of an explanation for this strange phenomenon.

Ben had his own theory: The motor was haunted.

Mr. Kropotkin swiveled his chair to face the second would-be inventor. "Well, Darren, let's hear about this project of yours that has you so confident."

"That's top secret," said Darren with a sly smile. "But don't worry, Mr. Kropotkin, it's finished, and it's awesome."

The teacher put down his notepad. "I'm going to need a little more than that."

"Well, I can tell you it has something to do with food."

"The sandwich has already been invented, Vader," Griffin put in sourly.

"You're hilarious, Bing," Darren drawled. "You should do more public speaking. Oh, wait—you've got that big speech coming up."

"That's enough," the teacher said tiredly. He began to make notes. "All right. 'Darren Vader—food-related.' Let's hope the finished product is more impressive than your description."

Good luck with that, Ben thought to himself. *A surprise invention from Vader. What could go wrong?*

On the other hand, Darren was looking a little pudgier than usual lately. Was that because he really did have a food-related invention — and maybe he was sampling too much of his own product? Did that mean his invention could actually be *good*? Could it beat Griffin and his haunted motor?

Mr. Kropotkin turned to the third and final inventor. "And how about you, Melissa? I hope you've got a little more information for me."

Pitch spoke up. "Good news. Melissa's invention is finished and tested, and we're ready to tell you anything you want to know about it — not like these *guys.*"

The teacher held up his hand like a traffic cop. "Are you Melissa's lawyer? Why can't she speak for this herself?"

So Melissa did. Or, at least, she tried. But her face stayed hidden behind her hair, and her voice was so breathless and terrified that the teacher couldn't make out a single word.

"All right, Antonia," Mr. Kropotkin finally relented. "You can speak for Melissa."

"It's called the Hover Handler," Pitch began enthusiastically. "It's a system to keep dogs from chasing cars." She took a folder stuffed with papers and diagrams and handed it to the teacher.

Mr. Kropotkin began to leaf through the papers, his eyes widening in surprise. "Melissa, this is *your* work?"

The shy girl nodded.

"Very impressive! I can't wait to see a demonstration."

Pitch leaned toward Griffin, Ben, and Darren, and mouthed the words: *In your face!*

At that moment, the door to the classroom was thrown open, and in staggered Savannah, sweaty and breathless, her expression wild. She looked like she'd run all the way from home, which was an awfully long way with the shortcut blocked.

"Savannah!" the teacher exclaimed in alarm. "What's wrong?"

"The Hover Handler!" she gasped, her voice raw. "It's gone!"

"What do you mean, 'gone'?" Pitch demanded.

"The exterminator's truck went by this morning!" she panted. "Luthor went after it like always . . . *and nothing stopped him*! He's okay. I got him back! But when I looked to see what was wrong with the Hover Handler, it wasn't there anymore!"

"Are you saying," the teacher asked, "that Melissa's Invent-a-Palooza entry has been *stolen*?"

"It has to be out in the open for it to work," Savannah explained. "Somebody must have just taken it!"

"Who would do that?" Ben put in. "I mean, you know it's a dog-saver, but most people wouldn't recognize it as something important. Unless it looks—you know—expensive—"

"Or maybe there are people who will want it out of the way so it can't kick their butts at the Invent-a-Palooza!" Pitch interrupted with a meaningful gaze at the boys.

Griffin stood up. "You're not accusing me?"

"Whoa, trouble in paradise," commented Darren. "I like it."

"Or this sleazoid," Pitch raged on, indicating Darren. "He'd steal fifty Hover Handlers if it could gain him any advantage!"

"Now, let's not jump to any conclusions," Mr. Kropotkin was saying.

Everyone in the room seemed to have an opinion, except for one person — Melissa herself. The Hover Handler's inventor had again disappeared behind her curtain of hair. But she had her cell phone to her ear and was speaking quietly.

"I know this is upsetting, Melissa," the teacher said gently, "but you know the rules. You can't use your phone in school."

"My parents are on their way," she told him in a voice that was emotionless and deathly quiet. "I want to go home."

11

OPERATION SHHHH!

Revised Objective: Eliminate POWER DRAIN side effect
1) Use lamp as EARLY WARNING SYSTEM

The instant the vacuum began to whir, the bulb in the test lamp winked out.

"Awww!"

In consternation, Griffin hit the off switch. Instantly, the bulb lit up again.

Ben sighed. "So much for the SH-2. It knocks out the power just like the SH-1 did."

"But why?" Griffin demanded. "It's not rocket science! I did it exactly right!"

"Well, at least the lightbulb showed us it was happening so we could shut down before anyone else was affected," Ben offered consolingly.

There were heavy footsteps on the basement stairs, and Mrs. Bing appeared on the landing. "How about a little warning before you turn on that Franken-vacuum?"

"Sorry," Griffin said sheepishly. "We haven't worked out the bugs yet."

"I'll give you bugs!" she raged. "I was just finishing a six-page e-mail to Grandma! Complete with pictures! And YouTube links! And it's *all gone!*"

Ferret Face chittered nervously under Ben's shirt. "He doesn't like confrontation," Ben explained apologetically.

"Then you'd better keep him out of this house," she snapped, "because there's going to be a lot of yelling until that project goes to school."

"It's not my fault," Griffin whined. "Even Dad can't figure it why it's doing that. He helped me rewire the whole thing, and it's worse than ever. And just when the girls dropped out, so the only person I have to beat is Darren—and how hard can that be?"

Mrs. Bing frowned her disapproval. "That's not very nice. I can only imagine how upsetting this must be for Melissa."

"I feel bad for them," Griffin admitted. "But that doesn't change what jerks they were before this hap-pened. Like I set out to make this a war between boys and girls. Pitch is the one who did that. And Savannah jumped on board the minute she found out Melissa's invention was about her crazy dog."

"In case you haven't noticed," Mrs. Bing said icily, "I'm a girl, too. Don't make me choose sides." And she headed back upstairs.

The boys were not far behind her. "This stinks," Griffin grumbled. "How are we going to fix it if we don't even dare turn it on?" He brightened. "Hey, maybe we can test it at *your* house."

"No way," Ben returned firmly. "If it shuts down our DVR and my mother can't record her soap operas, there'll be heads all over the place — including yours and mine."

Griffin was in the kitchen grabbing two Gatorades when a thump from upstairs captured his attention.

Must be Mom, he thought, but then he caught sight of her at the computer, retyping her lost e-mail, oblivious to everything else.

Ben had heard it, too. "Is somebody upstairs?" he asked. "Your dad, maybe?"

Griffin shook his head. "He's in the city today. It must have been a book falling off the shelf or something." Curious, he started up the stairs, Ben right behind him. Halfway up, they heard the sound of scrambling.

"Oh, boy," Griffin groaned. "If the squirrels are back in the chimney, my dad's going to freak."

But as they reached the top landing, he caught a glimpse through the open door of his bedroom and knew immediately that something was wrong. The contents of his closet spilled out into the room, his dresser drawers were pulled open, and his comforter had been tossed up onto the bed, as if someone had been searching underneath it.

Griffin and Ben ran into the room.

"No squirrel did this!" Ben whispered nervously.

More thumping sounds drew them back into the hall.

Griffin pointed. "The bathroom!"

The two raced into the white-tiled room and stopped short. It was empty. Griffin threw aside the shower curtain. Nobody there.

All at once, Ferret Face began struggling and flailing.

"Chill out, little guy!"

The pointy nose emerged from Ben's collar, and the beady eyes looked straight up.

Griffin and Ben craned their necks to follow the little ferret's gaze. There, in the narrow channel below the open skylight, hung Pitch Benson, caught in the act of making her escape.

"*Pitch?*" Griffin blurted. "What are you doing? We have a front door, you know."

Pitch jumped down, red with embarrassment. "Melissa's out of her mind," she said belligerently. "She can't believe what happened to the Hover Handler."

"The Hover—" Light dawned on Griffin. "You broke in and ransacked my room because you thought I stole the Hover Handler? What's the matter with you, Pitch? How long have we been friends—since kindergarten? You ought to know I'd never do anything like that!"

Pitch was shamefaced. "Sorry, Griffin. I wasn't thinking straight. I guess this wrestling thing really got into my head. So when the Invent-a-Palooza started up, I got down on you for treating Melissa like the B-team just because she's a girl."

"It never had anything to do with that," Griffin said earnestly. "To be honest, I didn't want to enter the contest at all, but everyone started putting all this pressure on me because of my dad. Like that makes me Thomas Edison. And then I made this stupid bet with Vader — it's my own fault, but I can't back out of it."

"I'm really, really sorry," Pitch repeated. She held out her hand. "Truce?"

Griffin shook it. "But only if you help me clean my room."

"Done. We can't be fighting. We've got Melissa to worry about. Griffin, I can't even tell you how destroyed she is by all this. She won't talk to anybody. She won't even come out of her house. Her folks are going nuts. I'm worried about her."

"Then we've got to do something," Griffin agreed. "That's more important than any dumb contest. We need a plan."

There was a quiet moan from Ben, who covered it up by clearing his throat.

Pitch nodded thoughtfully. "Normally, I'd run a mile, but I think you're right this time. Melissa's in real trouble. So what do we do?"

"Well, for starters, we have to figure out who took the Hover Handler," Griffin decided. "Maybe you had the right idea, but the wrong house."

She frowned. "The wrong house?"

"Seriously," said Griffin, "how could you possibly suspect me in a world that contains Darren Vader?"

12

OPERATION RECOVER HOVER

OBJECTIVE: To find who STOLE the Hover Handler and
GET IT BACK
PRIME SUSPECT: Darren Vader
POSSIBLE HIDING PLACES:
i) Garage
ii) Backyard shed
iii) Mr. Vader's boat . . .

"The boat's clean, Griffin," Pitch reported. "The only
thing I found there was a dead fish they forgot in
the refrigerator. Believe me, they're not going to forget it next season. They may never forget it as long as
they live."

Griffin crossed the boat off the list in his notebook.
"Are you sure there aren't any secret compartments?"

"Well I didn't have a lot of time to poke around in

there." Pitch rolled her eyes. "I had to hurry. Logan was annoying the harbormaster."

"Annoying?" Logan was wounded. "I was *acting*. I distracted him while you scoped out the *In-Vader*."

Pitch grimaced. "I don't think he believed you were a Swedish exchange student here from Oslo to study boats."

"I was totally in character," Logan insisted. "I had him eating out of my hand."

"He was laughing at you," Pitch shot back. "And by the way, Oslo is in *Norway*."

"It doesn't matter," Griffin put in quickly to keep the peace. "The important thing is no Hover Handler." He turned to Ben and Savannah, who had just emerged from the Vaders' backyard. "Anything in the toolshed?"

"Just lawn mowers and patio furniture," Ben replied. "We would have looked closer, but Savannah punched Ferret Face."

"I didn't punch him," Savannah said patiently. "I just gave him a tap on the nose so he wouldn't hurt that poor little chipmunk. That's how animals learn."

"He learned, all right," Ben returned bitterly. "He scratched the living daylights out of my stomach. You may be the big expert on dogs, but you don't know squat about the ferret world."

Savannah hung her head. "I can't even call myself a dog expert anymore. I'm powerless to stop my poor Sweetie from chasing that truck. We've got him locked in the basement now. If he has access to a window, he might go straight through it."

"Don't worry," Griffin encouraged. "When we get the Hover Handler back, he'll be golden. Did you get a good look inside the garage, too?"

Ben nodded. "I even looked under the cars and popped the trunks. Nothing."

"What now?" asked Pitch.

Griffin shrugged. "Vader must have stashed it in his house somewhere."

The five surveyed the gracious home across the street. It was one of the biggest houses in Cedarville, with a procession of windows on three different levels, indicating many rooms inside.

"Lots of hiding places in there," Ben commented bleakly.

"Not necessarily," Griffin countered. "He can't stick it in the middle of the living room or his parents will want to know what it is. That just leaves the basement and the attic. And, of course, his room."

"Yuck," put in Pitch.

"This would be so much easier if we had Melissa," Ben said with a sigh. "With a few keystrokes she'd take control of his computer and we could spy on him through his own camera. Or she'd hack into the security system and we could see the whole house. We'd have webcams in the windows and wireless microphones down the chimney, so we'd hear every word anybody says in there."

"I know it stinks to be without the kind of technology we're used to," Griffin admitted. "But you guys all heard Mr. Dukakis—Melissa won't see anybody. She won't even talk on the phone. She hasn't been in school for a week! If this keeps up, she'll go back to the way she used to be—too shy to whisper."

Pitch nodded. "Point taken. That's one of the main reasons we're doing this—to get Melissa's life back."

"Besides," Griffin went on, "if you've got the right plan, you shouldn't need fancy gadgets." He held up his paper with a flourish.

iv) the Vader home
STAKEOUT POSITIONS
PITCH: top of TELEPHONE POLE opposite house. Special equipment: BINOCULARS for distance view.
GRIFFIN: wooden LATTICE for climbing roses. Special equipment: PERISCOPE to look inside Darren's window.
BEN: CRAWL SPACE under front porch. Special equipment: STETHOSCOPE to listen through floor.
SAVANNAH/LOGAN: basement WINDOWS. Special equipment: FLASHLIGHTS.

Logan had a complaint. "You're under-using my talent. I could ring the doorbell and portray a friend calling for Darren."

"You're not that good an actor," Griffin told him.

"No offense. Nobody is. You'd have to pretend you can stand Vader."

Logan thought it over. "You may be right. Not even Johnny Depp could pull that one off."

"Okay." Griffin clapped his hands. "Places, everybody. For Melissa."

"For Melissa," they chorused.

The five started for their positions. But they'd barely gone a few steps when the front door opened and Mrs. Vader stepped out onto the porch to pick up the Sunday paper.

"Oh, hello," she said, a little taken aback. "Are you here to see Darren?"

13

The Man With The Plan was struck dumb, which did not happen very often. Mrs. Vader understood as well as anybody that her son and Griffin were hardly friends. On the other hand, what other explanation could there be for the five kids swarming on her property? She could not possibly know that her house was the object of a stakeout for a stolen Hover Handler.

Griffin finally found his voice. "Uh—is he home?" It wouldn't be smart to express his honest opinion of Darren to the one person who probably liked the guy.

"Yes, we're just about to have brunch," Mrs. Vader replied. "Why don't you kids join us? In fact, I insist."

Ben cast Griffin a stricken look and shook his head ever so slightly. The message was clear: *Please get us out of this.* Griffin, too, wasn't craving extra face time with Darren. But the opportunity was too great to pass up. Why peek in windows by periscope, hoping to catch a glimpse of the Hover Handler, when you could waltz right into the house as an invited guest and have a good look around?

"Thank you, Mrs. Vader. We'd love to. *All* of us," he added with a meaningful glance at Pitch, who seemed to be hiding behind the telephone pole she'd been about to climb.

They followed Darren's mother into the house, down the hall, and into the spacious kitchen. "Thank you for coming. We have so much food."

If the five team members were not thrilled to be guests in the Vader house, that was nothing compared with the look on Darren's face when they all trooped up to the table. "Mom—what gives? How come *they're* here?"

"Well, I don't think they're here to see Dad and me," his mother said reproachfully.

"Just be grateful they *are* here," grumbled Mr. Vader at the head of the table. "They can help us eat some of this—stuff."

That's when they caught sight of the brunch spread out on the buffet. There were poached eggs, scrambled eggs, fried eggs, frittatas, deviled eggs, eggs Benedict, omelets, and French toast.

"Man," commented Ben, awed. "You guys must really like eggs."

"Well," said Mr. Vader, helping himself to a deviled egg, "ever since the EGGS-traordinary came along—"

"Don't tell them, Dad!" Darren piped up urgently. "They're the competition!"

"Oh, Darren, it's the Invent-a-Palooza, not the Hunger Games," Mrs. Vader chided. "Where's the harm if your friends know that your invention is a self-feeding egg cooker?"

She pointed to the granite counter by the stove. There stood the EGGS-traordinary, a gleaming chrome tub. Everybody watched as an egg rolled down from a mesh hopper. It was cracked open by a tiny hammer, which jettisoned the shell and dropped the contents into the cooking mechanism. In barely a minute, a small plate of scrambled eggs came riding out on a conveyor belt, ready to eat.

"Wow, Darren, you made that all by yourself?" asked Savannah.

"Yeah!" Darren shot back belligerently.

"My law firm represents a small appliance company," Mrs. Vader explained. "They helped with the design and the manufacturing. But the concept was all Darren."

"So eat my dust," Darren added.

They all sat down to brunch. Even Ferret Face was given his own bowl of eggs Benedict under the table. Everybody had a hearty appetite, but they barely made a dent in the EGGS-traordinary's output. As the meal went on, Darren overcame his resentment at having his secret revealed and began to boast about his invention and how only a truly brilliant mind could have conceived of it.

"Yeah, I'd say I've got the Invent-a-Palooza pretty much in the bag," he concluded. "Nobody's going to come up with anything better than this. There's a speech in your future, Bing. I'll punch it up for you, so you don't bomb."

The scrambled eggs turned to poison in Griffin's mouth. He was dying to point out that not one ounce of this wondrous machine was Darren's own work. His mother's client had done the whole thing for him, complete with professional-grade manufacturing. But how could he say that in front of Mr. and Mrs. Vader when he was a guest in their home?

After brunch, Pitch sidled up to Griffin. "So what's the plan? Half of us keep the Vaders busy while the rest of us search the house?"

Griffin sighed. "Don't bother. Darren didn't steal the Hover Handler. Why would he? He's so confident that his egg cooker is going to blow the competition away that he doesn't even care about anyone else's invention. He's already got first place all sewn up."

"Yeah, you're dead meat," Ben added earnestly. "There's no way your dumb vacuum cleaner motor is going to beat that — even if you can get it to work."

"Come on," scoffed Pitch. "If Darren built that thing, I'm the Queen of England."

Griffin shrugged helplessly. "I know it. You know it. The judges will probably know it, too. And they'll still have to give him first prize."

They thanked the Vaders for their egg-cellent feast and took their leave.

"Later, losers!" called Darren at the door. His mood had really recovered since he'd encountered Griffin and the team in his kitchen.

"Well, I guess we don't have to bother looking for the Hover Handler anymore," Logan observed. "Darren's going to win the Invent-a-Palooza no matter what."

"Don't say that!" Savannah was almost in tears. "We have to find it for *Luthor*! I can't keep the poor baby tied up in the basement for the rest of his life!"

"And don't forget Melissa," Pitch added. "If she doesn't recover her invention, she'll never recover at all."

"So we have to get it back," Ben concluded. All at once, he shuddered from head to toe and peered inside his shirt. "Ferret Face, is that French toast? Who told you to take a doggie bag? It's sticky!"

"We're at a dead end," Griffin concluded glumly.

"What are you talking about?" challenged Savannah. "What about Operation Recover Hover? What about the *plan*?"

Griffin wheeled to face them. "Don't you get it? We don't have a plan—we have a mystery! If Darren doesn't have the Hover Handler, who does?"

Melissa was back at school, but she wasn't the same Melissa anymore. Her eyes never made an appearance at all. She did her schoolwork, yet even to teachers, her conversation was limited to a simple yes or no.

Griffin and the team made a huge show of welcoming her back. She acknowledged them with a slight wave and a barely audible "Hi." At the lunch table, their animated chatter bubbled around her, yet did not penetrate the wall she had constructed around herself.

"We're really sorry about that whole boys-versus-girls thing," Griffin told her earnestly. "We didn't mean for you to end up in the middle of it. I was wrong to be miffed when you entered the contest. It had nothing to do with you being a girl; I was just caught off guard."

"The whole thing was stupid," Pitch agreed. "And anyway, it's all over now. Honest."

A bit of sandwich disappeared into Melissa's hair and presumably reached her mouth.

Ben leaned in to Griffin's ear and whispered, "Don't mention the Invent-a-Palooza. That'll remind her about the you-know-what."

"Everything will remind her of her stolen invention," Savannah argued in a low voice. "If I talk about Luthor, she'll remember that the Hover Handler was created for him."

"I know a topic that's safe," Logan said enthusiastically. "The Ouch-Free Bandage Company has green-lighted my commercial! As soon as they hire a director, they'll be ready to start shooting."

A napkin entered the cocoon of hair, emerging a moment later, smeared with peanut butter.

Not even Mr. Kropotkin could get through to Melissa. The teacher begged her to start on another entry for the Invent-a-Palooza.

"It doesn't have to be as elaborate as the Hover Handler, Melissa. But this contest is tailor-made for you. You're so talented! Won't you reconsider?"

The answer, when it came from behind her hair, was a quiet, firm "No."

Every day after school, Griffin and Ben made their way to the Dukakis house, braving the long detour created by Mr. Hartman's fence. Each time, Melissa would refuse to come down from her room, using the excuse that she was "busy."

"Maybe she's working on a new invention," Ben

said hopefully. "Or rebuilding the old one. That would be good."

"She isn't," Mrs. Dukakis replied sadly. "She's just sitting there, staring at the ceiling. She hasn't turned her computer on in days."

Griffin and Ben were horrified. For Melissa, giving up technology was like giving up breathing.

"Her dad and I are worried," Mrs. Dukakis continued, her brow furrowed. "She was always quiet. But when she made friends with you kids, she really started coming out of her shell. I'd hate to lose all that progress because of this incident."

"Did you call the police?" Griffin asked. "After all, stealing is a crime."

"We did," Melissa's mother confirmed. "But because it was a school project, they're treating it as a prank. I don't think they're going to be much help."

Griffin studied his shoes. "We thought we had an idea who might have taken it, but we turned out to be wrong."

That was the most frustrating part of this. If Operation Recover Hover had been a true plan, they would have simply moved on from Darren to the next suspect on the list. But there weren't any other suspects. Melissa's only Cedarville competition had been Darren and Griffin. Of course, the Hover Handler had been completely out in the open in the Drysdales' front yard, so anyone could have taken it. But why? The device was unmarked and no one could possibly have known what its use was. It was too heavy for Cleopatra to move, and so bulky that Luthor could not possibly get his powerful jaws around it.

"Well, it definitely didn't walk away on its own," Pitch pointed out as they took the long way to school the next morning.

"We can't give up," Savannah pleaded. "Luthor trashed our basement last night because he heard the truck backfire. He tore the felt right off our pool table. My dad is beside himself!"

"You think I'm thrilled about it?" Griffin demanded. "Forget Melissa—if I can't stop my motor from turning off every light in the house, Vader's going to win the contest. He keeps revising the speech I have to give. Now he wants me to bring a tub of water and wash his feet in front of the whole school."

"So do something about it," Pitch urged. "You're The Man With The Plan!"

Griffin could only shrug. He found himself in a state that was equal parts uncomfortable and unfamiliar: completely out of ideas.

A ceasefire had been called between Savannah Drysdale and Ralph's Exterminators. The exterminator no longer accused Savannah of siccing her dog on him. In exchange, the girl promised to walk Luthor only during "safe" times when Ralph's truck was nowhere near Honeybee Street.

"I swear you must be the only middle school girl

who receives text updates from an exterminator," Mrs. Drysdale said in exasperation.

"Probably," Savannah sighed, clipping the leash onto Luthor's collar. "But I'd rather Ralph was in touch with me than with animal control. The poor Sweetie could end up in the dog pound for chasing cars — even if it's only *one* car."

Her mother frowned. "I wonder why he's so fixated on that particular truck. He doesn't go after anything else. Could it be the backfire that scares him?"

"If that was true, he'd be running in the opposite direction."

"Maybe the solution would be to let him catch it," Mrs. Drysdale ventured. "You know, to get it out of his system."

"I suggested that," her daughter agreed. "Ralph didn't go for it. He's afraid of Luthor, if you can imagine such a ridiculous thing. Like Luthor could hurt a fly."

Her mother smiled thinly. "Okay, not a fly. A pool table, maybe, but not a fly."

Savannah led her dog out of the house into the brisk air. She knew her mother thought she had a blind spot when it came to Luthor. Everybody felt that way. Well, that was their problem. They just couldn't see that he was gentle and sensitive and intelligent and kind. They were incapable of looking beyond his physical presence and gigantic teeth. Talk about judging a book by its cover!

As usual, Luthor led the way. Now that he was spending so much time in the basement, these brief moments of freedom were precious to him, and he leaped and ran, chasing the falling leaves and blasting through painstakingly raked piles, strewing their contents all over the lawns again.

"Oh, Luthor!" Savannah exclaimed, panting to keep up with him. "Don't you see the fun you could have if only you'd stop chasing that stupid truck! You're spoiling everything for yourself! And Dad," she added, thinking of her father holding up the green shreds of the pool table.

Luthor glanced back at her, utterly happy and eager to please. He was just about to make one of his bull runs, knocking her over and licking her face, when he stopped still, cropped ears pointing skyward. Then, suddenly, he was up on his hind legs, his front paws churning the air. It was strangely rhythmic, like a dance—

That was when she realized why all this was so familiar.

It was the hip-hop dance—the one Luthor always did when he chased the exterminator's truck and the Hover Handler was bringing him home!

Only there was no Hover Handler this time. Melissa's invention was gone.

She looked around to get her bearings. They were at the end of Honeybee Street where the former shortcut to school now stood behind Mr. Hartman's fence.

But if there's no Hover Handler, what's making Luthor act this way?

That was when she heard the high-pitched ringing sound, the Hover Handler's sonic tone. It was faint, muffled—the source must have been indoors. And there was only one house it could possibly have been coming from.

The meaning sank in swiftly.

We should have known! Why didn't we know?

Mr. Hartman had the Hover Handler!

15

I hate surveillance," Ben grumbled. "It seems like every time the wind blows, we're staking somebody out. I just got over my stomach cramps from surveillance on Vader. I think I might be allergic to eggs."

"We have to learn Hartman's habits," Griffin explained patiently. "We need to know when he goes out and for how long. We're not going to be able to get our hands on Melissa's invention if he's sitting there in the living room watching us break in."

Logan was not convinced. "I don't understand why we can't just call the police and get them to arrest Heartless for grand theft Hover Handler."

Griffin shook his head. "Melissa's family tried that already. The cops say you can't steal a school project— that it's just a prank. In their eyes, it's like taking somebody's baking-soda-and-vinegar volcano—not nice, but not criminal."

Pitch expertly shinnied down the trunk of the syca- more tree and dropped at their feet. "The webcam's in place," she reported.

"It's a good thing we had a few left over from the last operation," Savannah put in. "Melissa's totally out of commission. She won't even answer her phone anymore."

"She'll be herself again when we get the Hover Handler back," Griffin said confidently. "I'll send around the link so we can all monitor the camera on our computers and phones. With five of us checking, we should have most times covered."

"I can't make that kind of commitment," Logan informed them solemnly. "My commercial is ready to go into production. I could get a call from the ad agency any day now."

"Rehearse in front of the screen," Griffin advised him. "We need all eyes. We have to know every detail of Hartman's daily schedule, every move he makes. Like when he goes to the grocery store, how long does it take? Is it enough time for us to find the Hover Handler in his house? The difference between twenty minutes and thirty could be the difference between getting in and getting out, and getting in and getting caught."

Over the next few days, the team watched and waited. The live feed from the webcam rarely escaped scrutiny from at least one of the five. Griffin surreptitiously checked his phone during classroom breaks while at school; Ben woke up each morning and fast-forwarded through the overnight footage while serving Ferret Face his breakfast pepperoni; Pitch monitored the feed through a picture-in-picture window on her Xbox; Savannah recruited Cleopatra to keep an eye on the computer for her, and the capuchin monkey became as devoted to the video of the Hartman house as she was to her favorite TV channel, Animal Planet. Logan, too, was loyal, his eyes never far from the screen as he prepared for the most challenging role of his young acting career.

As the days passed, the team was forced to face up to a regrettable truth: They were no closer to learning Mr. Hartman's schedule because Mr. Hartman had no schedule. He never left the house — not to work, not to shop, not to exercise, not at all.

Ben was astonished. "I can't believe it. Coming out to yell at us is his only social life."

"And his only exercise," Pitch added. "He should weigh nine hundred pounds by now."

"He should," Savannah agreed in a hushed voice. "Have you seen the grocery deliveries that arrive at that house? There's no way one person can eat all that. He must be feeding a herd of elephants out his back door!"

"Maybe he's having a big party," Logan suggested.

"A party? That guy?" Griffin snorted. "Don't make me laugh. To have a party, you need at least one friend to invite. Heartless hates everybody, and I'm sure the feeling is mutual."

"Besides," Pitch added, "I've been watching those deliveries. They're not party food. It's all stuff in cans, like a lifetime supply of Beefaroni. Chef Boyardee must be buying a yacht."

Ferret Face's needle nose poked out of Ben's collar, sniffing the air. Beefaroni was one of his favorite snacks.

Ben pushed him back inside the shirt. "At least Beefaroni is edible. What do you think he's doing with all that wood?"

Five sets of eyes turned to the large pile of two-by-fours on the lawn of the Hartman home. Every so often, Mr. Hartman himself would appear, pick up an armload of lumber, and disappear into the house again. There was also Sheetrock, bags of cement, and bales of fiberglass insulation.

"I just figured it's some kind of Mr. Fixit project," Logan mused. "You know, home improvement."

"Yeah, but look at the home!" Griffin exclaimed. "It's not improving!"

"Maybe it is on the inside," Savannah suggested.

"No way," Griffin shot back. "We've all been inside Mrs. Martindale's house. You could knock the place down and rebuild it with the stuff he's hauled inside. That's concrete. You don't use it to fill cracks; you lay down foundations with it. He should at least be putting on an addition, but where is it?"

"Calm down," Pitch soothed. "What do we care what he's doing with those building supplies so long as we get Melissa's Hover Handler back?"

"The whole plan is based on surveillance," Griffin explained, his frustration evident. "When you can't explain what happened to five thousand pounds of lumber and a dozen cases of Beefaroni right under your nose, it means your surveillance isn't doing the job!"

All eyes turned to The Man With The Plan. If Operation Recover Hover wasn't working, he would know what changes needed to be made.

"So what do we do?" Ben prompted.

Griffin looked thoughtful. "If we can't *see* what's going on in there, maybe we can *hear* it."

16

The Drysdale house was a maximum-security prison. Pet gates had been installed in the doorways, and the simple act of getting from room to room had become a major operation of unlatching, opening, closing, and locking up again.

"It's for Luthor," Savannah confessed through tight lips and taut-skinned cheeks. "He knocked the basement door off its hinges, but the vet says the swelling in his nose should go down in another day or two."

Ben whistled. "If he busted a wood door, do you really think a few flimsy plastic gates can hold him back?"

"Not really," she admitted. "But they might slow him down long enough for Ralph's van to get out of range. Anyway, you get used to the inconvenience."

"Seriously?" called Mrs. Drysdale from the kitchen. "It takes me twenty minutes to carry a load of laundry upstairs. It's easier to get into Fort Knox than our bedrooms."

"It's only temporary, Mrs. D," said Griffin encouragingly. "We're working on it."

She frowned. "That doesn't mean there's a plan, does it?" She paused. "Don't answer that. I'll accept a plan if it means I can have my house back."

Savannah sighed. "It's been stressful on everybody," she confided once her mother was out of earshot. "The rabbits are getting claustrophobic. They can't hop high enough to see over the barriers."

Pitch looked around impatiently. "Where's Logan? He's been in there long enough to take a shower."

"I heard that," came a muffled voice behind the door. A moment later, Logan emerged into the hall and stood before their astonished eyes.

If it hadn't been Logan who had disappeared into the bathroom twenty minutes earlier, none of them would have recognized the person who had just stepped out. His short brown hair was now platinum blond and stood up in spikes. His face was ghostly pale, with black brows and dark-rimmed eyes. He wore a leather vest pierced with safety pins and no shirt at all. A temporary tattoo on one bony shoulder depicted a hooded cobra devouring a grinning skull. Loops of chain hung from his boots.

Savannah stared. *"Logan?"*

Ferret Face took one look and retreated back inside Ben's shirt.

Logan grinned. "Pretty good, huh? A true actor has to be able to transform himself." He dropped to the floor and tore off ten quick pushups. "To make my muscles pop," he explained.

"Your muscles wouldn't pop if you put them in the microwave," Pitch commented drily.

Savannah leaned forward, squinting. "Is that a *nose ring*?"

"If you're not willing to go all the way, you've got no place in show business," Logan declared in a nasal tone. His face twitched, and he sneezed violently. The nose ring flew across the room and pinged off the radiator.

"A clip-on," Pitch diagnosed. "Way to go all the way, Kellerman."

Logan went scrambling after it. "I wouldn't hesitate to pierce my nose for my art, but I've got the shoot for my commercial coming up." He retrieved the gold ring, blew off a fur ball from one or more of Savannah's many animal friends, and clipped it back to his nostril.

"I've got to hand it to you, Logan," Griffin approved. "There's no way Heartless is going to recognize you. Your own mother wouldn't recognize you."

"I hope not," Logan said fervently. "Because she'll kill me if she sees where I'm sticking her earring."

Ben frowned. "I don't get it. I thought Logan was supposed to be a delivery guy. How come he's dressed like a punk rocker?"

"A delivery guy is a *person*," Logan explained, "with hopes and dreams and a unique personality and style."

"And a clip-on earring hanging out of his nose," added Pitch in amusement.

"The point is," Griffin stepped in, "that when Heartless sees Logan, he'll be looking at the freaky stuff, not the face, which he might recognize as one of the kids he's kicked off his lawn."

"Actually," Logan informed him, "that's just a tiny fraction of my character—"

"Don't even think about it," Pitch cut him off. "Your job is to deliver the groceries, take a look around the house, plant the microphone, and get out."

"It'll be two-dimensional," Logan warned.

"That's fine," Griffin decided. "You'll win your Oscar when they turn the Ouch-Free commercial into a movie. Now let's get this done. Pitch, where are the groceries?"

"Just outside," Pitch replied.

The carton sat on Melissa's wagon, which had once carried the Hover Handler. Printed on the side was: 24 COUNT — OXTAIL SOUP.

"Oxtail soup?" Ben repeated. "That's a real thing?"

"It was on sale," Pitch told him. "If you wanted caviar, we should have chipped in more money."

"So long as it gets the job done," Griffin decided. "It's not like anybody's going to be eating it—except maybe Heartless, and he deserves it. Okay, Logan, you're on your own. The rest of us will be watching on Savannah's computer."

Logan puffed out his chest, jingling the safety pins on his vest. "In theater lingo, you tell me to break a leg."

"We're not going to do that," said Pitch nervously. "And be careful walking in those boots."

The carton of soup was heavy, and Logan was breathing hard as he made his way up Honeybee Street. He had abandoned the wagon a few houses back—Mr. Hartman might recognize it. Besides, it wasn't punk enough to go with the character he was portraying. His arms hurt like crazy, but of course that would make his muscles pop even more.

As he started up the front walk to the Hartman home he felt his heart pounding with the familiar exhilaration of a great role about to be brought to life. When he rang the bell, he was positively light-headed— although that might have been the exhaustion from carrying the soup so far. He made a mental note to join a gym so he'd be in better shape for these physically demanding roles.

And then the door opened and Mr. Hartman was scowling out at him. Showtime!

"Your groceries, man," muttered Logan in his deepest, sulkiest punk voice.

The homeowner's eyes narrowed. "I didn't order any groceries today."

Logan had prepared for this possibility. "Must be back-ordered from yesterday."

"I think yesterday's shipment was complete. What is this?" Mr. Hartman leaned forward and read the label. "Oxtail soup? I'd definitely remember ordering that."

"This is free, mister," Logan drawled. "It must be a bonus because you're such a good customer. I can carry it in for you. It's heavy." The last part required no acting at all. In fact, if Logan couldn't unburden himself of the carton soon, he was afraid his arms might snap off at the shoulder sockets.

The man continued to block his way. "Nothing is free in this world. Who sent you? The government?"

Logan gawked. "No, Maxi-Mart."

"Don't give me that! The government's everywhere!"

Logan's mind raced. A real actor had to be prepared for anything. But no one could have expected the conversation to veer in this direction. What did the government have to do with oxtail soup?

Stay in character, he reminded himself. Nothing could go wrong if he played his part to the best of his ability.

Lowering his dark brows over his mascara-rimmed eyes, he growled, "Mister, do I look like the president sent me?"

Mr. Hartman surveyed Logan over, from the platinum-blond spiked hair to the chains on his boots. "Make it quick," he barked finally.

To Logan, this was the equivalent of a standing ovation. He stumbled into the house on stiff legs — by this time, the strain of carrying the weight for so long had spread to his entire body.

His first thought was to search for the Hover Handler. It was nowhere in sight. The small house hadn't changed much since Mrs. Martindale had lived there. The walls were bare of her gallery of family pictures, leaving dark rectangles on the faded paint job. In the living room, her many decorative trinkets had been replaced by a clutter of boxes. Obviously, Mr. Hartman had been too busy hassling kids and fencing off their shortcut to unpack. Where that lumber and cement had disappeared to in this tiny place was anybody's guess.

Logan craned his neck to peer down the basement stairs. No sign of the Hover Handler there — and, strangely, no building materials, either. They'd seen Mr. Hartman carry a ton of the stuff into the house. Was he *eating* it? Obviously not, but then where was it?

Mr. Hartman stormed over to block his view. "Put the soup on the kitchen counter and scram."

Logan shuffled into the kitchen, eyes darting around desperately. Where could he plant the microphone? He heaved the carton up onto the counter with a groan of relief. Delivered! Now one more delivery: the mic. But how could he even take it out of his pocket with Mr. Hartman watching him like a hawk?

All at once, a new voice sounded from the open front door. "Delivery for Hartman."

Logan froze. Another delivery!

Mr. Hartman wheeled. "Not more oxtail soup!"

"No, sir. Cedarville Hardware."

"Oh, of course." As the homeowner turned to the door, Logan saw his chance. He jammed his hand in his pocket, pulled the miniature microphone out, and flicked the on switch, searching frantically for a place to hide it. In his haste, his half-numb fingers fumbled the tiny device, and it rolled off the counter and hit the tile floor with a *rat-a-tat.*

Mr. Hartman turned, startled. "What was that?"

Almost involuntarily, Logan reached out a toe and kicked the microphone under the stove. "Nothing, man," Logan grunted, getting back into his punk persona. "I'm done here. Thanks for shopping at Maxi-Mart." Satisfied that the performance was a success, Logan headed for the door just as the other delivery man came in, several boxes of nails balanced on his considerable paunch. Logan's painted eyebrows knit. Why was this new guy staring at him so intently? Could there be something in Logan's performance that didn't quite ring true? Was this the equivalent of a bad review?

Finally, the newcomer blurted, "How can you stand to look at yourself in the mirror every morning?" Logan was so startled that the hardware man added, "No offense, kid, but I honestly want to know. My boy went punk like you: the clothes, the hair, the makeup, the piercings—the whole Dracula thing. It broke up our family. His mother and I haven't talked to him in six years. So I have to ask: Why do you do it? Do you honestly think ghoul is cool?"

It took every ounce of Logan's acting ability not to look thrilled. Punks were never thrilled. But the thrill of having created a perfect character—that was a rare accomplishment for any actor.

Aloud, he replied, "Listen, man, this may seem weird to you, but it's my style, just like it's your kid's style, or those samurai guys who shaved the tops of their heads. It's a look; it's not the real person." Then, on impulse, he took an artistic risk. He removed the clip-on earring from his nose and held it out. "See? Underneath it all, I'm just the same as you."

The man set down his hardware and enfolded Logan in a giant bear hug. "I'm calling my son tonight," he declared emotionally. "Don't you think I won't."

"Great," said Logan, jamming the nose ring back in place before Mr. Hartman could see it was removable.

If I can come up with a performance like this in the Ouch-Free commercial, my career will be set!

*   *   *

"Can you hear anything?" asked Griffin urgently. "Did Logan plant the microphone?"

Savannah turned up the speakers on her computer. "I think so. There was a big crash and then some talking, but it's quiet now. I can't be sure. Melissa's so much better at this than I am."

"I hope Logan's okay," Ben worried. "What if that other delivery guy is from Maxi-Mart, too?"

"That would blow Logan's cover," Griffin agreed. He pointed to the screen, which showed their webcam view of the Hartman house. "Look—someone's coming out."

They watched as Logan and the hardware man started down the front walk.

"Wait," said Savannah with a sharp intake of breath. "Why is that man hugging Logan?"

Pitch shrugged. "It's the last thing *I'd* ever do."

The hardware truck drove off, and Logan disappeared from the webcam's range as he made his way down Honeybee Street. Griffin, Ben, Pitch, and Savannah rushed down to the porch to meet him.

"What happened?" Griffin hissed.

"My character," the young actor told him with satisfaction, "was spot-on."

"Who cares about your character?" Pitch snapped. "Did you see the Hover Handler?"

Logan shook his head. "No sign of it."

"What about the microphone?" Ben persisted. "Did you stash it?"

99

"Of course," Logan replied. "Well, technically, I dropped it and kicked it under the stove. But that's as good a place as any."

The group went back to Savannah's room to listen in. There seemed to be nothing to hear — no sound at all.

Griffin was worried. "Maybe the mic broke when it hit the floor."

"Or when he kicked it," Pitch added darkly.

They had the speakers cranked up so high that when the hammering started, it nearly shattered their eardrums. Savannah twisted the dial and turned down the volume.

"Savannah, what's all that banging?" came Mrs. Drysdale's voice from downstairs.

"Just a YouTube video, Mom." To the others, she whispered, "What's he doing over there?"

"He just got a new shipment of nails," Logan supplied.

"He's building something, but what?" Griffin wracked his brain. "What did you see?"

"Nothing. And how's this for weird — he thought I was from the government."

They stared at their friend with his spiked hair, eyeliner, nose ring, leather, and chains. How could anybody in his right mind believe that a middle schooler posing as a punk delivery boy might be from the *government*?

Griffin broke the stunned silence. "We'll keep watching and listening. Surveillance may be slow, but it always works. Sooner or later he'll let slip what he's doing with the Hover Handler."

18

For Melissa, the happiest time of every day was always the first eight seconds after opening her eyes in the morning. Second number nine was usually when she'd remember her invention, and the fact that it had been stolen, and nothing was right with the world.

True, she could have built another one — Savannah certainly wanted her to do that for Luthor's sake. But Savannah didn't understand. Nobody did.

Something that you invent with your own imagination, design with your own intelligence, and create with your own hands — that was more than just a *thing*. It was a part of you. No, more than that. It *was* you, indivisible from your very self. When the thief made off with the Hover Handler, what he'd actually stolen was a piece of what made Melissa uniquely Melissa. She could build a new machine, but that would not serve to make her whole again.

With a sigh, she sat up and swung her legs over the

side of the bed. "Power," she said aloud. Instantly, her room came alive with blinking lights and the whirr of computers, printers, and other components, humming their start-up songs. By the time she'd returned from the bathroom next door, face washed and teeth brushed, her favorite laptop was already downloading last night's messages:

GBingPlanner:
Operation Recover Hover in progress. Won't be long now.

NotSoBigBen:
Ferret Face misses you and so do I.

AnimalsRUs:
Please, Melissa. We need you. Luthor needs you.

GBingPlanner:
Did you just reply? SH-4 shut down power. Please resend message if there was one.

StageLogan:
You should have seen me @ Hartman's.
#readyformycloseup

MountainGirl:
Come back come back come back come back come back.

GBingPlanner:
Please re-resend. More SH-4 electrical problems.
Also could use your help designing SH-5.

Without changing expression, Melissa deleted all the messages, replying to none. Nor was she tempted to call any of her friends. These were the first people other than her family that she'd been close to. And where had that gotten her? Not that she blamed Griffin and the team. They certainly hadn't stolen anything. Still, she couldn't deny that life had been so much simpler when it had been just her and her computers. It made sense to go back to that simplicity.

She didn't want to be rude to anybody, and she wasn't. When her friends approached her in the cafeteria and asked if she wanted to join them for lunch, she replied honestly: "No, thanks." She thought she'd do better alone, as she always had before.

It was amazing how easy it was to get back into the old ways. Very few words were required, if any at all. A simple shrug or headshake was enough to decline most invitations — like being Savannah's lab partner in science, or hanging out after school. She didn't even have to deal with the others' disappointment. She just stayed behind her curtain of hair until whoever it was went away.

Of course, that hadn't stopped the e-mails or the phone calls or the text messages. And she was still greeted by dozens of Post-its on her locker every morning. But surely that would die out eventually. Not even The Man With The Plan could be *that* stubborn.

Her days weren't more fun this way, but they were safe and predictable. Already, when she saw Griffin and the others at their table across the cafeteria, it seemed like another life when she'd been a part of their group.

And yet they continued to leave her spot empty on the bench, an odd gap between Ben and Savannah. She could almost picture herself in it, with Ferret Face eyeing her jam sandwich enviously.

Well, maybe she missed that part just a little.

There was no question about it. Mr. Hartman definitely had the Hover Handler. Occasionally, the microphone Logan had kicked under the stove picked up the high-pitched whine of Melissa's invention and broadcast it over Savannah's computer. When that happened, the effect on the Drysdales' menagerie was nothing short of electrifying. Cleopatra would swing from the light fixtures. The cats, Rosencrantz and Guildenstern, would hide under blankets. The rabbits would try to cover their ears, which was no easy task. The turtles would splash muddy water all over their habitat. And down in the basement, Luthor would go into his hip-hop dance, laying waste to what was left of Mr. Drysdale's billiard room.

Mostly, though, the sounds that came from the

Hartman house were construction noises—hammering, sawing, and sanding.

The frustration was beginning to get to Savannah. "I thought you said surveillance works on everybody," she accused Griffin. "We've been watching this guy for more than a week, and listening in, too. We've got nothing."

"Surveillance works on everybody *normal*," Griffin explained. "Heartless isn't normal. He has no visitors, so there's nobody to talk to about the Hover Handler, or what he's building, or why he's stockpiling groceries. He never even uses the phone except to order more stuff. We might as well have thrown that microphone down the sewer."

Logan shook his head. "It wouldn't have worked. Dramatically, I mean."

There was a knock at the front door of the Drysdale house. Savannah opened it to admit a barely recognizable Pitch and Ben. They were covered from head to toe with a layer of fine dust. A powerful odor entered the foyer with them.

"Not so fast." Savannah backed them out onto the porch. "You can't come into the house all filthy and smelly. My mom'll kill us."

Ben was insulted. "That's the thanks we get for taking on a dirty job. Next time, *you* can go through Hartman's trash."

Griffin stepped forward on the porch. "What happened to you guys?"

"I'll tell you what happened," Pitch replied, her voice rising. "We opened the first bag and *boom*—it exploded!"

"He booby-traps his garbage?" asked Logan, stunned.

"No, he pulverizes it! All the paper was shredded and everything else was ground into mulch! First puff of wind and it's a blizzard!"

"Were there any clues in there about what he might be up to?" Griffin persisted.

"You must be kidding," Ben growled. "You see what's all over me? That's his trash! Ferret Face is coughing!"

"Seriously, Griffin," Pitch told him, "the only way to analyze this garbage is molecule by molecule. It's another dead end."

Logan was mystified. "Why would anybody bother to grind up their trash?"

"Who knows?" Griffin threw up his hands. "It's Heartless—the guy's certifiable! I've always said you can accomplish anything with a good plan, but Hartman is practically plan-proof!"

A collective gasp greeted this exclamation. It was a rare thing for Griffin Bing to admit that a problem might be beyond his powers of planning.

"Poor Melissa," Pitch lamented.

"Poor *Luthor*," Savannah added. "How could it be worse?"

* * *

By the end of the day, the battery in the wireless web-cam in the tree opposite the Hartman house had wound down. The video feed went dark.

"I can climb up there and plant a new one," Pitch offered, her mood somewhat improved after a shower and a change of clothes.

Griffin sighed. "Don't bother. We're never going to see anything watching the place from a distance. We need to get a good look inside."

"But that will *never happen*," Ben protested in a strident voice. "You said yourself that Heartless never goes anywhere. And we can't very well break in while he's home."

A needle nose poked out of Ben's collar and began sniffing experimentally.

Griffin looked suddenly thoughtful. "Maybe there's a way that we can get a look around in there and he won't notice."

"Heartless may be weird, but he's not blind!" Pitch exclaimed. "You're dreaming if you think one of us can get inside that tiny house without getting caught!"

"*I* can't," Griffin agreed. "And *you* can't." He smiled as the details of the plan began to come together in his mind. "But I know somebody who can."

19

OPERATION RECOVER HOVER
SPECIAL ASSIGNMENT: FERRETING OUT THE TRUTH

FIELD OPERATIVE: Ferret Face
MISSION OVERVIEW:
1) Strap small wireless WEBCAM onto agent's back.
2) Release agent BEHIND ENEMY LINES.
3) Monitor camera FEED by smartphone.

NOTE: Animal behavior EXPERT (Savannah) says ferrets cover a lot of ground when feeling threatened, so AGENT should run through ENTIRE Heartless home.

4) Perform AGENT EXTRACTION using PEPPERONI SLICES as bait.

OBJECTIVES:
a) Locate HOVER HANDLER inside Hartman house.
b) Discover the nature of SECRET CONSTRUCTION PROJECT.

Hold still, Ferret Face," Ben ordered. "Now put your left paw through here. . . ."

The harness was tiny. Savannah had first created it out of a Chihuahua leash so she could exercise her hamsters, but it had come in handy over the years. Now it was a perfect fit for Ferret Face, the wireless webcam fixed to his back.

Ben withdrew his hand to reveal an angry scratch along the back of it. He turned furious eyes on the little creature in his lap. "Do that again and you've tasted your last bite of beef jerky."

Savannah frowned at him. "We're asking a lot of Ferret Face today. You really should consider his feelings."

"He doesn't have feelings; he has claws," Ben shot back. "And they're sharp."

"A ferret is a carnivore, not a rodent," she reminded him. "It's not natural for him to be as passive as a hamster."

"He's a field agent," Griffin amended. "And without him, the plan is dead in the water. Get him suited up and let's do this."

"How come it has to be my ferret?" Ben complained. "He's not a pet, you know. He's a service animal, just like a Seeing Eye dog. Why not one of Savannah's hamsters or the mice or even Arthur?"

"Arthur's a pack rat," Savannah explained. "He'll go off looking for something shiny and never come back. The same goes for the rodents. They'll find what they consider a safe hiding place in the walls and stay there forever."

Ben was alarmed. "What if Ferret Face does that?"

"He's a hunter," she replied. "We can lure him out with meat."

Ben was forced to agree. "I guess you're right. He once chewed through a pizza box to reach the pepperoni."

"Let's just get this over with," Pitch urged.

Even from the front walk of 94 Honeybee Street they could hear the hammering going on inside the house. It wasn't loud exactly, but each blow carried its own vibration. For once, the noise brought them comfort instead of aggravation. As long as Mr. Hartman was working, they knew he wasn't watching his front door.

Griffin gingerly lifted the brass flap that covered the mail slot. Ben bent down, holding the ferret, camera and all, toward the opening.

Ferret Face turned to give his owner an uncertain look.

"It's called a plan," Ben informed him. "I wish I could tell you it's nothing to worry about. If you see a total jerk in there, give him a scratch from me. And be careful, little buddy." He dropped the furry creature through the slot.

Pitch was up next. As Griffin held the slot open, she squatted down, and, using a rubber band as a slingshot, fired a small piece of meat loaf deep into the house. Ferret Face was after it in a heartbeat.

They retreated across the street and ducked behind a hedge. Griffin produced his phone, and the team gathered around to peer over his shoulder. The screen was just a blur at first as the camera—mounted on the ferret's harness—whizzed through the house after the meat loaf projectile. That was followed by a moment of inactivity as the food was wolfed down. The webcam was pitched forward, so what they saw was practically a ferret's-eye view between two roundish ears.

"That's the living room." Logan supplied a play-by-play. "Wait—I think he's heading for the kitchen. That's where I kicked the microphone under the stove. . . ."

"Great," Pitch groaned. "He's decided to hang out in the only two parts of the house we already know the Hover Handler *isn't*."

"Don't worry," Ben said confidently. "Ferret Face is nosy. Sooner or later he'll cover every inch of that place."

It was true. Watching on Griffin's phone, the team was taken through room after room of 94 Honeybee Street. Between the furry ears they saw the master bedroom, where Ferret Face tried to make friends with a pair of fuzzy slippers. In the closet, he tore down several shirts and made himself a bed, only to decide he wasn't in the mood for sleeping.

In the bathroom, he climbed the wooden handle of Mr. Hartman's toilet plunger. He then jumped up onto the sink and helped himself to toothpaste but didn't like it very much. He didn't appreciate the shaving cream, either, and left in a huff.

His favorite part seemed to be the unpacked cartons that filled the living room and empty second bedroom. He played king of the castle on the highest ones and did a lot of jumping from box to box.

"Check out the basement," Griffin muttered under his breath as if the little animal could hear and understand. "The *basement*!"

"Only don't get caught," Ben added, stifling a yawn. His narcolepsy got worse during moments of stress, and now he had no ferret to administer the wake-up nip.

"Don't you dare fall asleep or I'll bite you myself," Pitch warned him.

In a utility closet, Ferret Face climbed in and out of an old briefcase at least a dozen times, and gave himself a massage by rubbing against a corrugated vacuum-cleaner hose.

"Get on with it!" Griffin urged.

"You can't plan what an animal is going to find interesting," Savannah lectured. "I think it's beautiful to watch his curiosity and imagination react to an unfamiliar environment."

"He's a ferret," Pitch reminded her. "He doesn't have an imagination."

"Not true," Savannah said stoutly.

"Then why can't he imagine himself in the basement?" Griffin complained.

It was another several minutes—although it felt like hours—before Ferret Face found the cellar door. They could tell by the bouncing motion that the discovery was very exciting. He descended in a series of leaps before losing his footing and tumbling to the bottom.

The picture disintegrated into scrambled pixels for a moment, and they worried that the camera might have been damaged. But the image was restored as Ferret Face righted himself at the bottom.

What they saw next canceled out all their relief that the plan was back on track. It was Mr. Hartman, looking down in shock and horror. A moment later, a large broom was coming at the camera at high speed. A split second after that, the picture degenerated into a turbulent blur.

"Nooo!!" wailed Ben.

"What happened?" asked Logan. "Is he dead?"

"I can't tell." Griffin stared at the screen, trying desperately to discern something concrete out of the chaotic images. He caught a flash of baseboard amid the tumult. "I think he's being chased."

"Run, Ferret Face!" Ben exhorted.

For the next few minutes, they were captivated by the wild jumble of distorted house scenes, punctuated by the occasional swipe of the broom. It was eerie, because it was all taking place on a tiny phone screen in complete silence. It was easy to forget that, for Ferret Face, this was a life-and-death struggle.

"Where is he?" Ben cried in agony.

"Is that the laundry room?" mused Pitch as a gleaming white appliance loomed up at them on the monitor.

"He's going to hit it!" squealed Logan.

"Duck, Ferret Face!" Ben bellowed.

Smack!

20

There was no sound, but they could all envision the violence of the collision. Images of the room tumbled after one another in rapid succession — ceiling, wall, floor, ceiling, wall, floor. At last, the picture stabilized on the base of the washing machine. A pair of feral eyes glowed out of the dark space underneath it.

"Of course!" Savannah exclaimed. "A small animal can flatten his body when he needs to hide!"

"But he couldn't flatten the camera," Pitch observed. "It must have been knocked off the harness."

Griffin slapped his forehead. "Who would have thought it could be so impossible to find one lousy Hover Handler in a two-bedroom house?"

"Never mind that!" Ben raved. "How are we going to save Ferret Face?"

"By following the plan, obviously." From his jacket pocket, Griffin produced a two-foot length of twine tied firmly around several slices of pepperoni. "Agent extraction, remember? Can Ferret Face smell pepperoni all the way from the basement?"

"Ferret Face can smell pepperoni all the way from Alpha Centauri," Ben assured him. "Come on. Let's get him out."

"It's too risky," Griffin informed him. "Heartless must still be looking for him. The last thing we need is to get caught dangling pizza toppings through his mail slot. We have to wait till the coast is clear."

"And how do we know when that will be?" Ben persisted.

"When he starts hammering again," Griffin supplied. "You can't spend your whole life chasing one little ferret."

At that moment, Savannah's cell phone rang. "Hello? . . . Oh, hi . . . Yes, Luthor's secure. You don't have to worry about him. Why? . . . Oh, really? . . ."

His mind focused on the extraction plan, Griffin ignored Savannah's conversation at first. But when all the color drained from her face, he began to pay attention.

". . . Okay, thanks for telling me . . . Bye." She ended the call.

Griffin frowned. "What's wrong?"

She swallowed hard. "That was Ralph, the exterminator. He always gives me a heads-up when he's going to be in our area to make sure Luthor isn't loose. Well, he just got an appointment on Honeybee Street — number ninety-four."

"*Hartman's* house?" Logan asked, mystified.

She nodded hopelessly. "The homeowner spotted a big, gray, long-nosed rat."

"That's *my* big, gray, long-nosed rat!" Ben exploded. "Why didn't you tell him not to come? That's no rat — that's Ferret Face!"

"She can't tell him that," Griffin reasoned. "How could she explain why she knows? Ralph would blab to Heartless that a bunch of kids planted a ferret in his house. The guy hates us enough already!"

"We've got to get Ferret Face out of there *now!*" Ben demanded. "An exterminator has sprays and traps and poisons! He's a professional hit man, a hired killer!"

"Right," agreed Griffin. There were times that risks must be taken because the plan had veered in an unexpected direction. Operation Recover Hover had to be put on hold. Getting caught was no longer their greatest worry. Rescuing the field agent had become Job One.

Griffin led the team back to the front door and, breathing a silent prayer, opened the mail slot and dangled the pepperoni rope inside. Ben pressed his face right up to the opening, hoping to see his furry friend approaching to take the bait.

No ferret.

"Maybe he can't come out because Heartless is right there," whispered Savannah.

"Maybe he doesn't like pepperoni anymore," Logan suggested.

Ben wheeled to shoot Logan a dirty look, jostling Griffin's hand. The brass flap of the mail slot fell shut with a clatter.

Everyone froze. In the urgency of the moment, the sudden sound was as loud as a gunshot.

It took footsteps inside the house to unfreeze them. Mr. Hartman was coming to investigate the noise!

Griffin yanked out the pepperoni lure and led the retreat to the cover of the bushes. Ben's sneaker slipped and he landed face-first in the flower bed. He was about to get up and run when the door was flung wide and Mr. Hartman stormed onto the walk. Ben crouched against the side of the porch and for once was glad he was small for his age.

The homeowner looked around. "Exterminators?" he called. "Ralph's Exterminators?"

Frowning, he advanced to the end of the walk and peered down the street.

Griffin watched in dismay as Ben unfolded himself from the flower bed, scrambled up the steps, and disappeared into the house.

"Oh, man," moaned Pitch, kneeling beside him. "Tell me I didn't just see what I think I just saw."

"He's rescuing his friend," Savannah whispered. "I'd do it for Luthor or Cleo or Arthur or any of them."

Mr. Hartman dialed his cell phone. "Hello, exterminators? I think you missed my house. I heard someone outside, but there's nobody here. . . ." His brows rose in surprise. "You're in Garden City? . . . So when do you think you can get here? This rat looks pretty mean. . . ."

At that instant, Ferret Face shot out the front door, ran right past Mr. Hartman, crossed the street, and disappeared into the bushes. The man could not have known that the little creature had been following the tantalizing scent of his favorite snack. He was safe in Griffin's arms, nibbling on the pepperoni rope.

Mr. Hartman laughed into the phone. "Never mind. Don't bother. The rat just took off. He's somebody else's problem now." He marched back inside, slamming the door behind him.

The sound seemed to echo around the bush, where Griffin, Pitch, Savannah, and Logan were exchanging anxious glances. All four were performing the same mental calculation: How panicked should they be? Was Ben trapped inside the house?

"Well, yes and no," Griffin answered everyone's unasked question. "I mean, he's stuck in there with Heartless. But all he has to do is wait till the guy goes to the bathroom and make a run for it."

Savannah nodded slowly. "I'll bet he's pretty scared, though."

"Probably," Griffin conceded. "On the other hand, he's been in plans before. He'll figure out what to do."

"Unless he thinks Ferret Face is still in the house somewhere," Pitch put in nervously. "He'll never leave without him."

"Good point." Griffin took out his phone and thumbed: *FF safe with us. Come out as soon as coast is clear.*

"What if Heartless hears the text tone?" Logan worried.

"Ben keeps his phone on vibrate," Griffin assured him. "Ferrets are sensitive to noise."

They waited, as Ferret Face picked the rope clean of pepperoni. The four sets of eyes never strayed from the door of 94 Honeybee. Ten very long minutes passed. No Ben.

"What's taking so long?" Pitch worried. "You think he's stuck in some closet with Heartless right outside?"

"Nah, that can't be it," Griffin told her. "Heartless has been moving around—you can see him through the windows. Ben should have had a chance to get out of there by now."

"So what could be stopping him?" asked Logan.

The explanation, when it came, landed on Griffin like a ton of bricks.

21

Ben was spelunking through a narrow mist-filled cave, trying to find his way to—

Where?

The answer was as elusive as the place he was trying to get to. He couldn't seem to focus. Why was he so groggy?

And why were his pants vibrating?

He reached around to his back pocket and his hand found the hard contours of his cell phone. It was buzzing against his hip. And that meant—

Reality returned in a series of bomb blasts, each one more devastating than the last. This wasn't any cave. He'd been asleep—a *narcolepsy* sleep! Why hadn't Ferret Face done his job?

He patted his shirt. The little guy wasn't there! At that moment, his bleary eyes cleared enough for him to take in his surroundings. He was in Hartman's laundry room, and his phone was ringing. He checked the display. *Bing, Griffin.*

He put the handset to his ear and whispered, "Griffin, what's going on? Where's Ferret Face?"

"Calm down," came his friend's quiet voice. "Ferret Face escaped. He's here with us. Everything's fine."

"For you, maybe!" Ben quavered.

"Don't get excited. Just wait till Heartless gets busy with something else. Then you can walk right out the front door."

"What if he decides to put in a load of laundry?" Ben hissed. "I'm sitting right in front of his washing machine!"

"We're directly across the street. I can see him through the window." There was a pause. "Uh-oh."

"Uh-oh?" Ben demanded. "What's that supposed to mean?"

"He's heading for the basement stairs. Hide!" Click.

Ben looked around desperately. As the smallest team member, he was the expert at getting into tight spaces, but the washer and dryer were pressed right up against the cement wall, and he couldn't move them without making a lot of noise.

He ran out into the main basement just as the footsteps began to sound at the top of the stairs. Oh, no! Heartless was already on his way down! Where could he hide? The furnace? No good—the boiler was right in the middle of the room.

Think!

He could see feet on the stairs. Another few seconds and he'd be face-to-face with the enemy!

His eyes fell on a half door. A storage closet? Even if it was a trash compacter, it was infinitely preferable to trying to explain to Mr. Hartman what he was doing here.

He made for it, ducking under the low frame, and tripping down three wooden steps, to roll on the sunken cement floor inside.

As afraid as he was, Ben couldn't help but check out his surroundings in amazement. This was no storage closet! It was a huge room, only partly finished, dimly lit by a bare bulb. He could tell immediately that this was not part of the original house. It was being excavated out of the ground beside Mr. Hartman's basement and finished with the concrete, lumber, and building supplies that had been delivered by the truckload.

At last, the truth was revealed of the mystery building project at 94 Honeybee Street. Mr. Hartman was putting a giant addition on the house—*underground!*

In fact, it seemed as if the place was going to get even bigger. The far wall was still dirt, and there were shovels and what looked like a jackhammer leaning against it.

The half door opened, and the stooping figure of Mr. Hartman ducked inside. Ben was galvanized into frantic action. He'd been so mesmerized by the discovery that he'd forgotten that catastrophe was only a few steps behind him! Out of options, he ducked between two rows of high wooden shelving and hunkered there in the shadows.

For a moment, Mr. Hartman was so close that Ben could have reached out and tripped him. But he passed untouched, proceeding to the end of the room, where he began running his hands over the unexcavated portion of wall.

Hidden amid the shelves, Ben crouched, trembling, taking in his surroundings for the first time. Every unit was piled high with canned goods — Mr. Hartman's parade of grocery deliveries. There was a vast variety of tinned meats, vegetables, pastas, soups and stews, jars of peanut butter, vacuum-sealed packages of crackers and cookies, dehydrated complete meals, and a seemingly endless supply of bottled water. There were enough supplies to feed somebody for years. A box contained dishes, cutlery, and several can openers. A folding cot leaned up against one wall. And . . . was that a toilet? What else could it be? The only difference was it seemed to flush by some kind of hand pump.

Was Heartless planning to *move* down here? Why? He had a perfectly good house right above, with a *real* toilet!

What was this place?

On the wall were pinned charts, maps, floor plans, and photographs of what looked like buildings at the center of heavily fortified fenced compounds. There were also newspaper clippings, headlines blaring: GOVERNMENT CONSPIRACY, BYE-BYE CIVIL RIGHTS, and IS UNCLE SAM PLOTTING AGAINST YOU?

Ben's head was spinning. Oh, sure, they knew Mr. Hartman had stolen Melissa's Hover Handler. They knew he was mean, unreasonable, unfair, and even weird. But nobody could have imagined he was this crazy. What kind of person moved underground like a mole, building a subterranean bat cave and filling it full of canned beans and cocktail weenies, not to mention strange maps and antigovernment newspaper articles?

A loud grinding sound filled the chamber, startling Ben out of his reverie. He dared a look. Mr. Hartman brandished the jackhammer-like device and was working away at the dirt wall. The thing was an excavator — it had probably dug out this entire room! The cutting blade reached a section of hard-packed earth, and the operating noise jumped several octaves to a high-pitched ringing.

The shock of that moment overpowered everything that had happened to Ben so far that day. The piercing whine was exactly the sound the girls had identified as the Hover Handler.

The noise coming from 94 Honeybee Street — the one that had made Luthor dance — had never been the Hover Handler. It had been this machine, digging the secret room.

With the screech of the excavator, and Mr. Hartman's back turned, Ben realized he'd never get a better chance. He sprang from between the shelves, nearly tripping over a can of oxtail soup, and scrambled through the half door to the basement. Then he was up the stairs, down the hall, and letting himself out of the house in a matter of seconds. By the time he crossed the street and joined the team in the bushes, he was moving at a speed that would have embarrassed an Olympic sprinter.

Ferret Face sprang into his arms and burrowed under his shirt in the blink of an eye. The other team members gathered around, anxious to hear his adventure.

"Are you okay?" Griffin asked urgently.

"Never mind me!" Ben panted. "I've got some news, and you're not going to like it." He paused to catch his breath, panning the group with wide eyes. "Heartless didn't steal the Hover Handler!"

22

Darren Vader's Invent-a-Palooza entry caused quite a stir when it arrived at Cedarville Middle School on Monday. The usual morning hubbub around the front entrance died as everyone watched Darren and his father ease the invention out of the back of their SUV.

There were oohs and ahhs as the two Vader men carried the central cooking tub with its mesh hopper, digital chronometer, and conveyor belt toward the building. The chrome exterior sparkled in the bright sunlight. The shapes and lines were sleek and well-designed. Everything about the device screamed professional grade. Darren had added a stainless-steel plate engraved with the words *EGGS-traordinary by Vader.*

"What is that thing?" asked Kate Mulholland in a hushed tone. "A satellite?"

"It looks like a miniature nuclear reactor," put in Marcus Oliver.

"If you think Vader's got the brains to invent something like that, you're about as smart as he is," Griffin said in disgust. "It's an egg cooker—like there's no such thing as a frying pan and a stove."

"That's still pretty cool," Kate remarked. "I mean, look at it. It's beautiful."

"Vader didn't build that thing," Griffin scoffed. "One of his mother's clients did."

"'Scuse me, guys," Darren was saying. "Invent-a-Palooza winner coming through." He stopped in front of Griffin. "Hey, Bing, you want to memorize the speech, or should I put it on cue cards?"

"The contest isn't over yet," Griffin told him through clenched teeth.

"It kind of is," Darren offered in mock sympathy.

"There's still plenty of time before the Long Island finals."

"I know," Darren acknowledged. "I'm just giving the teachers a little preview of *EGGS-traordinary by Vader*. You know, before it's too famous to bring to school without security."

"Isn't your dad an inventor?" Marcus asked Griffin. "You should be awesome at this."

"My entry will be here soon," Griffin said defiantly. "Count on that. I'm just putting a few finishing touches on it."

"Come on, Darren," Mr. Vader said impatiently. "Let's get this to Mr. Kropotkin so I can go to work."

Burning with resentment, Griffin watched the gleaming EGGS-traordinary disappear into the school. It was beyond infuriating. Vader was going to win the contest with an invention somebody else had built for him. And all because Melissa's Hover Handler had been stolen by—who knew? Not Mr. Hartman, that was for sure. He turned out to be just a bad neighbor and a crackpot.

As for Griffin's Invent-a-Palooza entry—that was a very sore point. He'd developed a virtually silent motor—the sound-muffling was even more effective than before, thanks to a square of theater curtain, provided by Logan. The material was just as fire retardant as Ben's bunny-rabbit pajamas, since it had to meet the state code for opera houses and concert halls. But the electrical problems were as bad as ever. Mr. Bing had hosted the last meeting of the Nassau County Inventor's Guild so he could pick his fellow members' brains. Nobody could explain why the Bings' vacuum cleaner was knocking out electricity all around itself while continuing to run perfectly.

One of the guests had suggested that the problem was in the Bing house, not the machine. So Griffin had tested the SH-5 at Pitch's. Not only had the invention plunged the Benson home into darkness, it had also made the streetlights flicker and initiated rolling blackouts up and down the block. One of the victims had been Logan, three doors up. He'd been halfway through blow-drying his hair for the filming of the Ouch-Free commercial when the power surge had caused the dryer to blow a capacitor in his hand. Luckily, he hadn't been shocked. But facing the cameras with imperfect hair could permanently damage Logan's career. The young actor had made a point of saying that if anything bad happened it would be all Griffin's fault.

What could Griffin do? He'd gone home to start work on the SH-6.

The EGGS-traordinary was a huge sensation around the school. Mr. Kropotkin featured it in every science class. During the three lunch periods, the aroma of cooking eggs wafted out of the faculty lounge, and contented teachers could be seen smacking their lips and patting their stomachs all day. Darren was a celebrity, strutting through the hallways, accepting praise and congratulations, and bragging about how he would win the Invent-a-Palooza at the county and state levels, before going on to sweep the national finals.

"He's going to be impossible to live with," Pitch complained, watching Darren sign an autograph for a seventh grader. "I mean, he's *always* impossible, but this is worse."

"At least you didn't bet on it," Griffin said bitterly. "I'm the one who's going to have to make a speech."

"This is so unfair," Ben lamented, slipping a slice of breakfast sausage under his collar to Ferret Face. "The Hover Handler could beat that stupid egg thing in a fair fight."

Griffin hung his head. "Operation Recover Hover is done. I know a dead plan when I see it, and this one is six feet under."

"But what about Luthor?" Savannah protested. "If we can't get the Hover Handler back, my parents are going to make me buy a shock collar. Can you imagine that? I'd be putting a portable torture chamber around my best friend's neck!"

"And what about Melissa?" Pitch added. "She's gone back to the days when she was a hermit who never talked to anybody. We're *losing* her!"

Griffin shrugged miserably. "We have to face facts. We ended up on two wild-goose chases, and lost the trail completely. I'd love to keep searching, but there are no leads. Melissa's invention could be anywhere by now. For all we know, it's buried in some garbage dump, or halfway around the world. We'll never find it."

"What are the odds that Hartman's digging machine would sound exactly like the Hover Handler?" Ben lamented. "Just our luck."

"What are the odds that Mrs. Martindale would sell her house to a crazy person?" Pitch demanded. "Who hollows out Carlsbad Caverns to move into? You know, unless you're an earthworm . . ."

"I've been thinking about that," Griffin mused. "Remember what Heartless asked Logan that time: 'Are you from the government?' And he had antigovernment news articles on the wall. What if he's one of those guys who's convinced the government is out to get him? You know those photographs and floor plans he has? I'll bet they're government buildings he's suspicious of."

"Maybe that's why he got so freaked when we tested the Hover Handler," Savannah added. "He's probably obsessed with secret drones spying on him."

"That still doesn't explain why he's building an underground room stocked with groceries," Logan pointed out.

"Actually, it kind of does," Pitch said. "If you're wacky enough to think the government is plotting against you, what do you do? You build a shelter where no one will be able to find you. And you stock it with tons of supplies so you can survive there for years, or even longer. It makes perfect sense—if you're completely paranoid, I mean."

Savannah sighed. "Poor Mr. Hartman."

"Poor Heartless?" Ben choked. "Spend an afternoon trapped in his dungeon before you say that."

"I'm serious," Savannah persisted. "At first I thought he was just mean. But he's really nuts."

Pitch nodded. "You're right. It can't be fun to be totally out of touch with reality."

"If they ever make a movie about Mr. Hartman," Logan said with relish, "I'd love to play that role. I do crazy like nobody's business."

"Stick to 'ouch,'" Pitch advised.

"That's *yeow*," Logan informed her, "and I nailed it. Filming went great—no thanks to Griffin and his stupid vacuum cleaner."

"I guess I feel bad for Heartless, too," Ben conceded grudgingly. "Digging yourself an underground hiding place—that's a pretty creepy thing to do."

"Save your sympathy for *us*," Griffin advised. "It's one thing when your plan hits a snag. That's happened plenty of times. But when there's no plan at all, it doesn't matter how smart you are, how motivated you are, or even how desperate you are—a dead end is a dead end."

The others regarded him in dismay. It was shocking to see The Man With The Plan admit defeat.

Savannah had gone to bed in a terrible mood. She woke up feeling even worse.

Normally, the busy a.m. routine at the Drysdale house energized her. Today, she sleepwalked through it. She dumped feed into cages, barely even looking at their inhabitants, and tossed Cleopatra her breakfast plantains like it wasn't important to greet a friend. Even Lorenzo, her albino chameleon, was given his teaspoonful of dead flies without so much as a kind word. Rosencrantz and Guildenstern seemed to be objecting to the state of their litter box, but she chose to ignore them. This was risky; when Rosencrantz and Guildenstern complained about the litter box, the next complaint usually came from Mom.

She regretted treating everybody this way. Nothing was more important to Savannah than animals. To her, they were not pets, but full-fledged family members. That was exactly why she was so upset this morning. The errand before her weighed heavily upon her heart, but she'd promised her parents.

It was shock-collar day for Luthor.

The whole idea of it went against everything Savannah had ever believed in. This was so-called "invisible fencing," where the poor Sweetie would receive a painful jolt of electricity whenever he passed a certain perimeter. In theory, after enough nasty shocks, the dog would learn not to leave the yard, even if the red truck was right outside, backfiring past their front door.

The thought of deliberately causing an innocent animal pain seemed like the ultimate cruelty to Savannah. Luthor would not know why his collar was suddenly tormenting him. And when the pain went away, he wouldn't understand that, either. This "invisible fence" might succeed in keeping him out of the road, but who knew what damage it might inflict on his spirit? Luthor appeared ferocious to some, but Savannah knew how innocent, and trusting, and childishly sweet he was. If this impersonal instrument of torture robbed him of his warm and loving nature, Savannah would never forgive herself.

Oh, how she longed for Melissa's Hover Handler. No pain, no shock, just a natural reaction to a high-frequency sound. It was 100 percent effective and 100 percent humane. It was sheer genius, just like its inventor. No, it was beyond genius; it was *art*. And like so many great artists, Melissa had been unable to accept the idea that her creation had been stolen.

Poor Melissa. Poor Luthor. What a disaster all this was turning out to be.

The simple act of clipping the Doberman onto his leash nearly overpowered Savannah with guilt. To take him along on the mission to purchase this horrible device seemed like the ultimate betrayal. She sighed. At least there was no chance of running into the exterminator's van. Ralph himself had confirmed that he was working in the city today and wouldn't be back until well after dark.

Savannah rode out of town on her bike, Luthor loping along beside her at the end of an expanding leash. Pet Galaxy was on Route 31, a mile or so beyond the town limits. Route 31 was wider and busier than the quiet Cedarville streets, but Luthor was under control, keeping pace with her in the bike lane.

And this magnificent, well-behaved animal needed a shock collar? What a joke!

No sooner had the thought crossed her mind than she glanced over her shoulder, and Luthor was *gone*!

No—that wasn't right. His hind end was still back there. Where was the rest of him?

Savannah squeezed the hand brakes so suddenly that she nearly catapulted herself clear off the seat. She abandoned the bike and wheeled to face her beloved dog.

He was up on his hind legs, swaying from side to side, his head bouncing, his front paws churning rhythmically. It was the Hover Handler dance!

But the Hover Handler was gone, and Mr. Heartless's excavator was more than two miles away!

Then it was over, and Luthor was back to normal, as if nothing at all had happened. Savannah ran to him, stooping to gather his gigantic head into her embrace.

"There, there, Sweetie. Everything's fine."

Of course, everything *wasn't* fine, and Luthor could sense it. Or maybe his keen animal intuition was picking up on her confusion. What had brought about this latest episode of dancing? She'd heard no high-pitched ringing this time, but that might have been the traffic noise. Luthor's hearing was much sharper and more selective. What was loud and clear to him, a human might miss completely.

So what had caused it? What were the odds that someone around here was using the very same kind of excavating machine that Heartless had in his secret room? She looked around. There was no construction going on — at least nothing she could see. Of course, Mr. Hartman had been digging underground, but why would an established store or restaurant do that?

Her pulse quickened. What if this wasn't an excavator or some other power tool that made a similar sound? What if it was the real thing — the Hover Handler itself, in the hands of the thief who had stolen it?

She did a three-sixty, standing right there on the shoulder. On the opposite side of the road there was a Vietnamese restaurant, a florist, a bike repair shop, a hardware store, and a barber on the corner. On this side there was only one thing. It was a—

What was it?

It was so different from the rows of shops and eateries along Route 31 that Savannah was amazed she'd never noticed it before now. Maybe that was because it was just very—*overlookable*. It was almost as if someone had dropped a humongous gray shoe box in the middle of a Long Island field. It was about four stories tall with very few windows and no noticeable features at all. The fence around the property was at least twelve feet high and covered with warnings:

DANGER
HIGH VOLTAGE
DO NOT TOUCH

The only break in the perimeter led to an entry gate. As Savannah watched, a car nosed in, presented ID at a gatehouse window, and was admitted by an automatic barrier that swung wide. There were only a few cars in the parking lot. Whatever this place was, business was not exactly booming.

There must be a sign somewhere, she reasoned. But, aside from the high-voltage advisories, the only identification she could find was a small plaque on the gatehouse, declaring this to be FACILITY 107-B.

"What's that supposed to mean?" she mused aloud.

Luthor had no answer. He was hip-hop dancing again.

Savannah reached for her phone.

24

"I hate Route Thirty-One," complained Ben as he and Griffin pedaled single file out of Cedarville onto the main road. "The traffic noise makes Ferret Face antsy."

"Ferret Face will get over it," Griffin tossed over his shoulder. "Stay behind me in the bike lane. Savannah's just up ahead."

Ben knew there was no turning The Man With The Plan from his course. Ever since Savannah had called twenty minutes ago, he had been like a bloodhound that had picked up a scent and was planning to follow it to the ends of the earth. It was big news. If there was a chance that they had not completely lost the trail of the Hover Handler, Griffin was going to be on it, dragging the team with him.

They biked on for another ten minutes before Ben spotted Savannah, waiting for them by the curb. Luthor was with her, on his hind legs, in the throes of the dance. No wonder she had smelled Melissa's lost invention.

As they cycled up, the big Doberman dropped back down to all fours. He seemed surprised to see Griffin and Ben at first, and greeted them with an unfriendly growl before returning his attention to Savannah. His huge liquid-brown eyes looked up at her in appeal, as if to ask, *If you can't fix this, could you at least explain it to me?*

"Did you see that? That's the fourth time Luthor's been dancing." Savannah explained her theory that the Hover Handler must be somewhere inside the mysterious Facility 107-B. "I think they might be *testing* it in there, or at least trying to use it for something. But what?"

Griffin frowned. "I can't believe I've never noticed this place before. We all must have driven by it a thousand times."

"I know, right?" Savannah agreed. "It's practically on our doorstep. Another mile and it would be inside our town limits. How have we overlooked it all these years?"

Ben couldn't stop staring at the nondescript gray structure. He was unable to shake the feeling that he'd seen it somewhere before. Driving by? It was possible, but he didn't think so. The image in his mind was not the building itself so much as a *photograph* of the building. But that didn't make any sense, did it? And the name — Facility 107-B. That rang a bell, too. He could picture the letters and numbers scribbled in blue ink on masking tape. The makeshift label was under the photograph on a wall. But what wall?

Ben thought hard. It was rough, unpainted—unfinished Sheetrock. The lighting was harsh—a bare bulb. A stack of canned goods stood on a shelf nearby. A label came into focus in his mind: DELUXE OXTAIL SOUP.

When the answer came to him, he let out an "Ohhh!" that sounded almost like a groan of pain.

"What is it?" Griffin asked.

"I just remembered where I've seen this building before," Ben said faintly. "It's on the wall of Mr. Hartman's secret room."

His best friend was surprised. "What—this place? Are you sure?"

Ben nodded. "It's not just the building; it's the name. He had it marked *Facility 107-B*. How many of *those* could there be?"

"But Mr. Hartman is a conspiracy nut," Savannah protested. "All the stuff on his wall is about government installations he doesn't trust."

"Could *this* be a secret government installation?" Ben wondered. "I mean, it's secret enough. We all grew up near it and never noticed it before. But what would they be doing with Melissa's Invent-a-Palooza project?"

Griffin's eyes were alight with discovery. "It makes perfect sense! Melissa's so smart that she must have invented some piece of technology for the Hover Handler that the government wants!"

"But why would the government *steal* the Hover Handler when they could just phone Melissa and ask her how it works?" Savannah asked, bewildered.

"It must be classified information, so they can't admit what they're going to use it for," Griffin concluded.

"Are you telling us that Heartless has been right all along?" Ben demanded. "If the government would steal from a middle school kid, who knows what else they might do? Maybe we should all be digging underground rooms and laying in supplies of oxtail soup."

"It doesn't matter," Griffin said firmly. "It doesn't change the plan."

"The plan?" Ben echoed. "You said the plan is dead."

"Only because we lost track of the Hover Handler," Griffin replied reasonably. "We thought Vader had it, and we were wrong. Then we thought Heartless had it, and we were wrong again." He watched as Luthor's big black-and-tan body rose up on its hind legs for another dancing session. "But this time we know exactly where it is."

25

OPERATION RECOVER HOVER–PHASE 3

PRIME SUSPECT: THE POWERS THAT BE
OBJECTIVE: Get inside Facility 107-B and TAKE BACK
what's RIGHTFULLY ours. . . .

Pitch peered over Griffin's shoulder at the plan on his desk. "Aren't you forgetting something? If the government thinks Melissa's invention is important enough to steal and keep inside a top secret building, don't you think they'll make it pretty hard for anyone to sneak in there and jack their stuff?"

"It's not *their* stuff," Griffin pointed out. "It's *our* stuff. Melissa's stuff, anyway. It's no different than taking back a million-dollar baseball card."

"Except that the baseball card wasn't being guarded by SEAL Team Six," Ben reminded him uneasily.

"SEAL Team Six has more important things to guard than an unmarked warehouse across from a barber shop," Griffin retorted. "You saw that place, Ben. It's not like it's crawling with security. They've got a gate-house where they probably ask you to show ID. Our own parents have to do that to get into our school."

"Our school doesn't have an electric fence," Logan noted.

"So it's a little more secure," Griffin continued. "The important thing is we're in the right. That's *our* Hover Handler. Our friend invented it, and it was stolen right off our other friend's front lawn."

"Luthor needs it," Savannah added. "And Melissa."

Griffin nodded. "We can do this. All we need is the right plan." He picked up the pen and added to the page:

PROCEDURE:
Step 1 . . .

Ben snatched the pen from his hand. "Don't even bother. I already know. Surveillance, right?"

Griffin laughed. "No surveillance. This time the surveillance has already been done for us."

Pitch stared at him. "By who?"

"By Heartless," Griffin replied readily. "He knows every secret government installation in a hundred-mile radius. Ben, you yourself told me he's got pictures of this place and a whole map and floor plan."

"Yeah, but that's in his house. Technically, *under* his house." Ben's face registered dawning horror. "We're not going back there! It's too dangerous! Look how I got stuck last time!"

"That was a breakdown in planning," Griffin conceded. He took his pen back and wrote:

Step 1: Gain ACCESS to Heartless's BASEMENT:
(i) create a DISTRACTION
(ii) Heartless runs OUTSIDE
(iii) team ENTERS premises undetected

"What distraction?" Pitch challenged.

"There's only one that will get Heartless out of his house," Griffin replied confidently. "Kids trespassing on his precious property."

The steam from the soup fogged his safety goggles, and Ezekiel Hartman took them off so he could see his lunch. Oxtail soup—he hadn't ordered it, but he was beginning to develop a taste for the stuff. It was *strong*—just what he needed to keep his energy up after a long morning working on the safe room.

It was almost ready. He'd completed the last of

the excavation. All that remained was the rest of the Sheetrock and a few finishing touches. If the government came to spy on him and intrude into his life, he could survive down there for years.

He took another sip, enjoying the burn of the strong broth, and that was when he saw it—out of the corner of his eye, through the kitchen window. It was one of those kids—those trespassing schoolkids who were determined to get their shortcut back. There she stood, bold as brass on his property, working at the fence with wire cutters!

Dropping his spoon with a clatter, he dashed out of the kitchen, flung open the front door, and raced into the yard. "You, there! Get away from my fence!"

The girl wheeled, watched him rush toward her for a few seconds, and then took off like an antelope. Mr. Hartman was hot on her heels, matching her stride for stride.

She was younger and faster, but—still running, he frowned—every time she opened a lead, she'd slow down a little, keeping him in the hunt.

She was *toying* with him!

At last he pulled up, breathing hard. Rotten kid! Bad enough to vandalize his fence, but did she have to lead him on a chase all around the neighborhood?

He turned back to his house, noting in perplexity that his front door was wide open. He could have sworn that he'd closed it behind him when he'd burst outside. He began to jog home. At least the fence didn't seem to be damaged. He must have disturbed that awful girl before she could use her wire cutters.

Back in the house, he locked the door and returned to his lunch. The soup had cooled off, and he was carrying the bowl to the microwave when he heard a muffled thump from downstairs.

Someone was in the house!

He grabbed the nearest available weapon — a frying pan — and stepped out into the hall. He could hear whispering on the basement steps.

His safe room — the government must have found it!

He bustled to the top of the stairs and froze. Kids again — two boys!

"Don't hit me!" Ben pleaded. "There's an innocent ferret in my shirt!"

Mr. Hartman goggled at the needle-nosed creature staring out from the intruder's neckband. It was the rat! Was the government training small animals to do its dirty work now? And kids to be their handlers? That girl with the wire cutters must have been the decoy to lure him from the house so they could get access to his basement.

"We can explain," said Griffin.

For the first time, Mr. Hartman noticed the rolled-up poster in the bigger boy's hand. He snatched it away and opened it. It was the map and floor plan of Facility 107-B from the wall of the safe room!

"Do you know what this is?" he demanded.

Griffin nodded. "It's that building out on Route Thirty-One with no signs and an electric fence."

"And what's it to you? Why do you need my blueprints?"

The two boys were tight-lipped and silent.

"Who sent you?" Mr. Hartman persisted.

"Nobody," said Ben in surprise.

If they were lying, they had been well trained. They seemed genuinely scared to death, especially the smaller one with the rat.

Griffin sighed in resignation. "Our friend's invention got stolen, and it's being held in there."

The story the boys went on to tell was absolutely bizarre. And yet, he had seen this Hover Handler with his own eyes! A drone copter that made the big dog dance!

"Are you telling me," Mr. Hartman said, lowering his frying pan, "that the *government* stole that machine?"

The boys studied their sneakers.

"I know it's kind of hard to believe," Griffin mumbled.

"Are you kidding?" Mr. Hartman crowed. "It's as plain as the nose on your face! Of course the government stole it!"

"So," Griffin forged on, "we were hoping to *borrow* the floor plan so we could, you know, break in and steal it back."

Mr. Hartman regarded them for a long moment. Then, "It seems that I've misjudged you fine young people."

It was the boys' turn to stare.

"It's your duty as citizens to stand up for freedom and take back what's rightfully yours," Mr. Hartman told them in a strident tone. "I'm with you all the way!"

Griffin and Ben gawked at him in astonishment.

"You mean," Griffin said at last, "you're going to let us borrow the blueprints?"

"I'll do better than that," Mr. Hartman promised. "I'm going to lead this mission. Now what we need is a plan."

Ben gulped. "You've come to the right place."

26

The pet gates were still up, turning the Drysdale home into a complex maze. There was no sign of Luthor.

"Where's the dog?" asked Pitch.

Savannah sighed. "I'm keeping him in the basement."

"But isn't the shock collar supposed to stop him from chasing the exterminator's truck?" Logan queried, frowning.

"It would," Savannah said tersely. "It would also give him a nasty shock. There's no way I'm letting *that* happen."

"So why bother buying it in the first place?" asked Ben.

"Because I promised my parents he'd have a shock collar. Fine, he has one. But if you think I'm going to let that awful thing fry my Sweetie, you're out of your mind. I'm keeping his *regular* collar in my pocket every minute. The instant I can get rid of that instrument of torture, you can bet I will."

"We understand," Griffin told her. "Luthor's lucky to have an owner like you."

"Family member," she corrected firmly.

"Right," he amended. "Anyway, Ben and I have to tell the rest of you about a change of plan. It might be a little out of left field. We're going to have an extra team member for this phase of the operation."

Pitch opened wide eyes. "Melissa? Did you get Melissa to come back? Griffin, you're a genius!"

"No, it's not Melissa," Ben told her sadly. "And wait till you hear—"

The doorbell cut him off.

Mrs. Drysdale answered it. "Oh, hello there." She sounded surprised. "Is there something I can do for you, Mr. —?"

"Hartman," came the reply. "I'm here for the meeting."

"Heartless?" croaked Savannah. "What's he doing at my house?"

"He's with us now," Griffin supplied.

"Oh, sure," said Pitch. "Three weeks ago he put up a giant fence just to keep us from crossing his precious lawn. He hates our guts."

"That was before he found out the government stole the Hover Handler," Ben explained. "He's got a serious hate on for the government."

"That's why he's going to help us," Griffin added. "It never hurts to have an adult on the team. Adults have *cars*."

"Savannah, your—friend is here to see you." Mrs. Drysdale ushered Mr. Hartman into the living room. Her eyes narrowed. "What's this 'meeting' about?"

Savannah was struck dumb, so Griffin filled in the silence. "Well, we kind of got off on the wrong foot with Mr. Hartman here, so we want to work on our, um, neighborliness."

Mrs. Drysdale looked to her daughter for confirmation. Savannah nodded.

"Neighborliness," Mrs. Drysdale repeated faintly. "That's a good thing. I hope I won't have to hear any more complaining about shortcuts and fences."

The phone rang, and she rushed off to answer it.

Savannah watched her go, then turned back, annoyed. "Now my mom is suspicious. Thanks a lot, Griffin. Why did the meeting have to be here?"

"Well, it definitely couldn't be at my place," Mr. Hartman informed her. "The government has the whole house bugged."

Pitch was unconvinced. "Are you sure? Why would the government be so interested in a random person living in a random Long Island town?"

The newcomer reached into his pocket and produced a tiny wireless microphone. "Look what I found under my stove. If the government didn't put it there, who did?"

Logan went into a violent coughing spasm. Pitch pounded him on the back hard enough to knock him off his chair.

"Well . . ." Griffin began reluctantly. His usual pol-
icy was to never confess to things adults didn't already
know. But it would only hurt the plan if Mr. Hartman
put two and two together halfway through Operation
Recover Hover. "That was us. We thought you took the
Hover Handler, and we were trying to find out where
you were hiding it. Our bad."

Mr. Hartman thought it over. "It's still the government's fault. You never would have suspected me if
they hadn't stolen your friend's invention in the first
place."

The five middle schoolers exchanged uneasy glances.
No one was comfortable teaming up with Mr. Hartman,
who was at least a little bit crazy. What kind of person
saw a conspiracy behind every rock? On the other hand,
in this case, he was right. The stolen Hover Handler
was in a government building; who could have stolen it
but the government?

"If that facility is so top secret," Ben asked timidly,
"how did you get a map of it?"

Mr. Hartman motioned them all closer and dropped
his voice. "I'm not alone," he said to the huddle. "There
are quite a few of us who don't believe everything
Washington tells us. We meet on the Internet and share
information—maps, charts, documents. I spent all of
2012 watching Facility 107-B from the Vietnamese restaurant across the street. It wasn't easy, because I can't
digest spicy food, but that's what the government is

counting on—that regular citizens won't have the will to suffer a little heartburn to stand up for their freedom."

"And what did you learn?" Griffin prompted.

"A lot of white coats pass through that security gate," Mr. Hartman replied. "Military uniforms, too—mostly brass. I think it's a government lab—high-security clearance—because everything that goes in and out travels by armored truck."

Ben nervously stroked Ferret Face, who became restless during long conversations. "I don't like the sound of that. It's one thing to sneak into some guy's basement—no offense, Mr. Hartman. But this is like taking on the army. A bunch of kids can't do it. Nobody can."

"Don't be so quick to give up," Mr. Hartman advised. "I agree it would be impossible to get in there during the day. But every night, they lock the place up and go home."

Griffin pounced on this. "Are you sure? What time exactly?"

Mr. Hartman shrugged. "Saigon Palace ends their early-bird special at seven, and by seven thirty, all the squints and brass hats have left the lab. Even the sentry chains the gate and moves on."

Savannah spoke up. "There's no fence Pitch can't get over, no matter how high."

"Aren't you forgetting something?" Ben reminded her. "High voltage? Keep out? That's an *electric* fence."

"It's true," Mr. Hartman confirmed. "The busboys at the restaurant used to throw leftover noodles at it, just to watch them fry."

"Well, there's no way we can get in during the day, when the place is full of scientists and soldiers," Griffin concluded. "We have to find a way to get past that fence."

Pitch shook her head sadly. "I'll climb anything, Griffin. But not if it's impossible to touch it."

"And we can't very well camp out on Route Thirty-One, waiting for the next power failure," Ben added.

"I guess not," Griffin conceded glumly. "Unless . . ." When the expression on his face began to change, it was almost as if a miniature sun had come out to shine exclusively on him.

The team recognized that look and sat forward expectantly.

Even Mr. Hartman could sense that something was coming. "What is it, kid?" he prompted. "Unless . . . ?"

The Man With The Plan beamed all around the room. "I think I might know a way we can make our own power failure."

27

OPERATION RECOVER HOVER

FINAL FIELD PLAN
Rendezvous Point: 94 Honeybee Street (HARTMAN house)
Zero Hour: 12:15 a.m.
Wheelman: Mr. HARTMAN . . .

For Ben Slovak, the experience was eerily familiar: sitting up in his bedroom waiting for his parents to go to sleep so he could slip out of the house undetected.

It wasn't easy being best friends with The Man With The Plan. The sneaking around, the close calls with disaster, and, occasionally, an actual disaster. Long lectures from parents, teachers, and the police replayed themselves at high speed through his nervous mind. Even those scrapes with the law seemed minor compared with what they were up against in Facility 107-B.

The United States government. The armed forces. Men and women with guns, who were dedicated to protecting this nation from all enemies, foreign and domestic. Including Griffin Bing and his marauding band of middle schoolers.

Most familiar of all was the fear—the lump in his throat, the gnawing in his stomach, the jelly feeling in his legs. And, of course, the vicious cycle of dozing off from sheer stress only to be brought right back into the tension and misery by Ferret Face's wake-up nip.

It had already happened three times tonight before his parents finally turned off the TV. Next came the tricky part: skulking outside their half-open door listening for signs of sleep. Times two. Mom snored, so if she fell asleep first, it was practically impossible to hear Dad over the noise.

Straining, he was able to detect his father's steady breathing underneath Estelle Slovak's buzz saw. He timed ten minutes to be absolutely certain, and then tiptoed downstairs. Silently, he shrugged into a jacket and eased himself out the back slider.

From his collar, Ferret Face looked up questioningly, as if to ask, *It's dark. Where are we going in the middle of the night?*

"It's a plan," he whispered in reply. "We're doing it for Melissa, and for Luthor. And even a bit for Griffin, so he doesn't have to give that speech. Courage, Ferret Face."

The little animal opened his mouth, revealing his needle-sharp teeth. He didn't need courage. He needed pepperoni. Ben slipped him a slice. "Make it last. We might be in for a long night."

Griffin huddled in the bushes at the end of the block.

Ben indicated the long, thin duffel bag thrown over his friend's shoulder. "Is that what I think it is?"

Griffin nodded. "Let's go. They're waiting for us at the rendezvous point."

Keeping to the shadows, they started in the direction of the Hartman home. Most of the houses were dark. All was quiet. They turned right and started up Honeybee Street, passing the Drysdales' on the left. The only sign of life was at the end of the block, number 94. There, Ezekiel Hartman, dressed all in black like a burglar, complete with stocking cap, entertained a very uncomfortable Savannah and Pitch.

". . . and that's why I threw out my waffle iron," Mr. Hartman finished. "So the government couldn't use it to beam secret brainwashing messages at me."

"Guys, are we ever glad to see you!" Pitch breathed. "We were just—uh—hanging out with Mr. Hartman."

"Where's Logan?" asked Ben.

"Late," Savannah replied nervously. "We thought he might be coming with you."

Pitch was impatient. "I say we go without him. It's not like we need an actor to impersonate the secretary of defense if we get caught."

"He probably just got held up somehow," Griffin decided. "We'll swing by his house on the way."

Mr. Hartman left home so seldom that none of the team had ever seen his car. They watched in amazement as a gigantic Jeep Wagoneer from the 1970s backed out of the tiny garage, clearing the door frame by half an inch on either side. Waving their arms to disperse the cloud of blue exhaust, the team piled in, Griffin and Ben dragging the long duffel.

The driver eyed it in the rearview mirror. "Is that—?"

Griffin set the bag at their feet. "The special equipment," he confirmed.

A trip to Logan's house turned out not to be necessary. They encountered the young actor running full tilt up Honeybee Street.

"Sorry I'm late," he panted as Griffin hauled him aboard the Wagoneer. "The DVD of my commercial came in, and we watched it twenty-seven times. My folks just got to sleep a few minutes ago."

"I'm surprised it didn't put the whole family to sleep," Pitch commented drily.

"Are you kidding? My 'yeow' would wake the dead!"

The streets were mostly empty. They encountered very few other vehicles as Mr. Hartman guided his ancient Wagoneer through the town of Cedarville. Route 31 was busier, but still relatively quiet. Even the Saigon Palace was dark and deserted at this hour. That was where they parked the Jeep—behind the building, next to the Dumpster that smelled of chili oil.

"Don't even think about it," Ben advised Ferret Face, who was becoming agitated at the food odor.

As they scampered across the four-lane road, the shadow of Facility 107-B came into focus, and the enormity of what they faced hit them with full force.

"I wish we didn't have to do this," Savannah said in a small voice.

Mr. Hartman was outraged. "Did the Sons of Liberty chicken out at the Boston Tea Party?"

"Did the British have an electric fence?" Ben countered.

They reached the opposite sidewalk and stared up at the chain-link barrier. It towered over them, twelve feet high. The sentry booth was unoccupied, but the main gate was chained and padlocked. The only other way in was a metal emergency door, wired into the rest of the fence.

Logan, who had sensitive ears, was aware of a low power hum, and Ben was sure that a jittery Ferret Face could hear it, too.

Pitch opened her water bottle and squeezed a splash at the fence. A few tiny sparks appeared around the wet links. "It's live, all right," she confirmed.

Griffin set down his duffel and opened the zipper.

Mr. Hartman stared. "A vacuum cleaner?"

"Trust me, Mr. Hartman. This vacuum cleaner is the enemy of electricity everywhere." He took a small tool kit from the duffel, knelt at the base of the nearest streetlight, and began to unscrew the access panel.

Then he reached in with cutters, snipped two wires, and attached the open ends to the prongs of the vacuum cleaner's plug. He took a deep breath. "Here goes nothing."

"It would be just our luck if this stupid thing worked properly for the first time ever," Ben said nervously.

Breathing a silent prayer, Griffin flicked the switch on the vacuum.

The team and Mr. Hartman crowded around as the machine hummed to life—not the usual roar of the motor, but the pleasant whir of Griffin's Invent-a-Palooza project. The SH-9 was even quieter than the previous SH models, with its three layers of theatrical curtain fabric. In a way, it was an amazing success. Every round of refinements had reduced the operating noise that much further.

The one thing Griffin had been unable to do was to fix the sole side effect, that last little kink.

Now he needed that kink more than he'd ever needed anything in his life. . . .

28

The streetlights winked out first, for at least a quarter mile in both directions along Route 31. The neon signs on the storefronts were next. The barber pole stopped turning. The temperature readout in front of the bank went dark. The clock stopped. Far beyond them, Long Island was still open for business. A plane passed overhead; somewhere, a train whistle blew. The sky reflected the glow of lights in the distance all around them. But they were surrounded by darkness — that and the gentle purr of the SH-9.

"Whoa!" breathed Pitch. "*This* is your Invent-a-Palooza project?"

"I was just trying to make the motor quiet," Griffin admitted. "I don't understand the power part. Nobody does."

"If I didn't know you brought that thing here," said Mr. Hartman with respect, "I'd swear it was a government conspiracy."

"Listen!" Logan rasped. "The fence — it's not humming anymore!"

Pitch hefted her water bottle. "Excuse me if I need a little more proof than your ears." She lobbed another squirt at the chain link. No sign of sparks. The electric fence was dead.

Leaving the quiet motor still running, Griffin arranged the duffel bag over the vacuum. In the darkness, it was unlikely that a passing motorist would spot it there against the base of the streetlight. Still, it paid to be careful.

Climbing like a monkey, Pitch clambered over the high fence and let herself down the other side. In short order, she had the emergency door open from inside the compound. One by one, the team members and Mr. Hartman entered the grounds of Facility 107-B.

Griffin already had the light from his phone trained on the map of the complex. "There's an entrance around the side," he whispered. "It's the best way in and out."

They scampered around the corner of the building and entered a recessed area invisible from the road. Griffin tried the door. Locked.

Mr. Hartman went to work with a set of lockpicks. Perspiration began to trickle down from his stocking cap as he probed and twisted.

The team members exchanged nervous glances. This was taking a long time. What if they couldn't get in?

At that moment, there was a click and the door swung wide. Mr. Hartman flashed them a triumphant smile. "Score one for the good guys."

The team didn't feel like good guys; they felt like burglars. If it hadn't been so urgent to get back the Hover Handler, none of them would have attempted something so crazy.

Six phone lights panned the darkened reception area. All found the placard above the main desk:

UNITED STATES GOVERNMENT
FACILITY 107-B
NEW TECHNOLOGY ASSESSMENT
AUTHORIZED PERSONNEL ONLY

Ben's eyes were drawn to a security camera pointed straight at them. "Oh, no!"

"Calm down," Griffin soothed. "See? No red light. Those things run on power and there is none." He stepped up to a door that was protected by a badge scanner. It pushed open at his touch. "The electronic locks are off, too."

A large carpeted area partitioned into a maze of work cubicles stretched before them.

"Man, this place is big," observed Savannah in a worried tone.

"And there are four floors," Logan added. "How are we ever going to find the Hover Handler in all this?"

"We'll split up," Griffin decided. "Half of us will start at the top and work our way down; the others will start from here and work up. Surely we'll find it before we meet in the middle."

Ben, Savannah, and Mr. Hartman took the stairs to the fourth story. With no electricity, the elevator was out of service. The layout was identical to the main level — endless work stations created by a system of room dividers. Searching all of them — times four — was going to be no small task.

Mr. Hartman paused at the entrance to the first cubicle. "I hope you kids are prepared for what you're about to see. It's bound to be plenty disturbing, considering the government went to a lot of trouble to keep it secret."

They peered inside. A half-eaten cheese sandwich sat on the desk, next to an open thermos.

"It looks like somebody's lunch," Savannah commented, stepping inside the office.

"Don't touch it!" Mr. Hartman rasped. "The cheese could be plastic explosive and the thermos could be filled with biological agents!"

She sniffed. "Soup. Split pea."

Ben put a firm hand over the restless bump in his shirt. Why did it always have to be food? "We can't waste time," he urged. "We're looking for one thing, and soup isn't it."

Yet as they continued to investigate the rows of offices, they found nothing in this top secret government facility that might not have appeared on the desks of an accounting firm or a mail-order address-label business. There were family photos, handicrafts obviously made by kids, *#1 Dad* mugs, plus random paperweights, letter openers, and even a plaque for coming in second in the pie-eating contest at the CIA holiday party.

When they finally stumbled across some technology, it turned out to be a chrome appliance that resembled a space-age sewing machine.

"Stay back!" ordered Mr. Hartman. "It could be radioactive!"

Ben shone his phone light at the paper on the desktop beside the device. "It says here it's an automatic baseball stitcher. Guaranteed to put a hardball in your glove in three minutes."

Mr. Hartman's brow furrowed. "What would the government want with a baseball stitcher?"

"Maybe they're fans," Ben suggested.

"There must be some other reason. But what?"

They moved from cubicle to cubicle, finding examples of technology that were even more puzzling: a solar-powered salad spinner; a toothbrush with a built-in cell phone; an ergonomic bicycle-tire pump; a laser-operated bagel slicer with Toast-As-U-Cut™; self-propelling ice skates.

With each discovery, Mr. Hartman grew more frustrated. "Where's the spy equipment? Where's the poison gas?"

"We're looking for an invention that keeps dogs from chasing cars," Ben pointed out. "This stuff fits right in."

"If it's going to protect the lives of beautiful animals like my Luthor," Savannah said sharply, "then it's a lot more important than anything as lame as poison gas."

"There's nothing up here," announced Mr. Hartman, his voice stiff with disappointment. "Let's head down to three. That's probably where they keep what they *really* don't want us to see." He headed for the stairwell.

Savannah and Ben followed.

Ben checked his watch. They'd been inside Facility 107-B for fourteen minutes already, and so far, no Hover Handler.

"I hope Griffin's having better luck than we are," he whispered to Savannah.

29

I hope the others are having better luck than we are," murmured Griffin. "There's nothing here but gadgets and junk."

Pitch peered into yet another cubicle. "Ha—looks like some kind of corn popper."

"Looks like?" Logan echoed. "Is it or isn't it?"

"Who cares?" she replied. "If it's not a Hover Handler, it's dead to me."

They headed to the second floor and started all over again, their flashlight apps probing into the darkened offices. No Hover Handler.

"This has to happen soon," Pitch warned. "My phone's already under twenty percent. If our lights give out, we'll never find the exit. We'll be stuck here until the day shift shows up to arrest us."

"Let's hope the others still have phone power," Griffin said grimly. "It's our only means of communication."

"Guys!" Logan hissed urgently. "Over here! Quick!"

Griffin and Pitch raced in the direction of his voice, colliding not once but twice in the dark hallway. They came upon Logan crouched over a desk, his eyes luminous with discovery.

"Where is it?" Griffin cried. "Where's the Hover Handler?"

"I don't know," Logan replied. "But look at the picture. This guy took his family to Universal Studios!"

"The next time you get our hopes up like that, *you're* going to Universal Studios," Griffin growled. "Straight through that window."

Pitch reached over to the shelf and snatched the first thing she could get her hands on, with the intention of hurling it at Logan's head.

"Freeze!" Griffin ordered in a half-demented scream. He shone his light at the object Pitch was holding.

It was a shallow metal box, topped with an X-shaped superstructure. At the tips of the X were four miniature rotors.

"You found the Hover Handler!" Logan exclaimed.

"Is the stand there, too?" Griffin croaked.

"Got it!" Pitch pulled the base from the shelf, unplugged it, and tucked it under her arm. "Call the others and let's get out of here!"

Griffin began to punch at his phone.

"Aha!" Mr. Hartman pounced on the shiny black device and held it up triumphantly. "Now you're going to see what the government doesn't want you to know about!"

He brandished the rifle-like apparatus by the front and rear grips, aimed it at a blank section of wall, and squeezed the trigger. A thick reddish-brown liquid shot out of the nozzle and put a fine coating on the paint.

Instantly, Ferret Face was out of Ben's shirt, scratching at the baseboard and licking at the drippings as they streamed down to the floor.

"Kid, get your rat!" Mr. Hartman urged. "It's probably toxic!"

Savannah read the name from the paperwork on the desk. "Bar-B-Baster." She sniffed "Barbecue sauce?"

Ben scrambled after his ferret. "Cut it out, Ferret Face! You know spicy stuff gives you hiccups!" He scooped the little animal up and stuffed him back under his shirt, leaving dark stains on his collar.

Mr. Hartman was red as a lobster. "Barbecue basters! Eyelash curlers with Wi-Fi! Wind-powered lawn mowers! What is this — a joke? There's not a single piece of technology in this whole building that could hurt a fly!" Totally dejected, he sagged into an office chair, arms folded in front of him.

Snap!

A heavy belt shot from each side of the seat. The two halves whipped around his waist and met at his lap, clicking firmly together in what looked like a metal buckle. With a whirring sound, it cinched tight, pinning him in place.

"What the—?" Mr. Hartman tried to pull the two pieces apart. The buckle seemed to be locked. Then he began to wriggle in an attempt to work himself free. The belt permitted him zero motion. "I'm stuck!"

Savannah and Ben rushed to his side and tried to yank on the belt in order to loosen it. The mechanism began to whir again.

"Stop it! Stop it!" Mr. Hartman howled. "You're only making it tighter!"

"But how are you going to get out?" asked Savannah breathlessly.

At that moment, Ben's phone rang. He let go of the belt and answered it. "Griffin?"

"We've got the Hover Handler," came his friend's voice. "Meet us at the exit right now."

"We have a little problem—" Ben started to say. But a click told him that Griffin had already hung up. He turned to face Mr. Hartman and Savannah. "They've got it."

Savannah sighed with relief. "Luthor will be so happy!"

"I'm overcome with joy myself," Mr. Hartman said sarcastically, "but I happen to be stuck in this chair."

Savannah produced a small nail file and began to saw at the fabric of the belt. "Don't just stand there," she told Ben. "Help me."

"But . . ." Ben protested. How could he possibly cut through the strap when he didn't have anything sharp? He ransacked his pockets and came up with a wad of plastic wrap. At the very center of this was his last piece of pepperoni. It dawned on him—he *did* have something sharp. He pulled out the meat and rubbed it on the seat belt. Then he removed Ferret Face from his shirt and pointed his long nose in that direction. "Smell that, buddy? Go to town."

Obligingly, the little ferret began to gnaw at the fabric with his needle-like teeth.

"At this rate, I'll be out by Christmas," Mr. Hartman said nervously.

"We're working as fast as we can!" Savannah never looked up from her sawing.

"Don't panic, Mr. Hartman!" Ben exclaimed, struggling to control his own trepidation. Griffin, Pitch, and Logan were probably waiting for them at the entrance by now. The only comfort was that none of them could leave without Mr. Hartman, since he was their driver. "No rush—"

At that moment, a loud electronic bleep sounded throughout the building, and a recorded voice announced:

Initiating backup power-generating system in five—four—three—two—one—

The lights flickered once and came on full. Facility 107-B hummed to life.

Mr. Hartman reached under his stocking cap and pulled a full ski mask down over his face and head. "Quick!" he urged. "Hide yourselves! The cameras will be live again!"

Ben could feel his cell phone vibrating in his pocket—Griffin, asking where they were and why they hadn't shown up yet. There was no time to answer.

And anyway, how could he even explain what was delaying them? *Well, Ferret Face isn't done chewing through the seat belt on the evil government chair that attacked Mr. Heartless.* Yeah, that said it all.

He pulled his T-shirt to his nose like a bandana and signaled to Savannah to do the same. "Hang on, Mr. Hartman!" He rolled the swivel chair out of the office and began to push his passenger down the hall. "The elevator!" he hissed. "With the backup power on, it should work now!"

Savannah abandoned her sawing and ran alongside them. Ferret Face continued to gnaw at the pepperoni-flavored seat belt.

Mr. Hartman was jubilant. "How do you like that, Uncle Sam? We're getting away! And we're taking your stupid chair!"

"We're only taking it because it's attached to one of us," Ben puffed, just in case the cameras had microphones attached.

"Wait!" Mr. Hartman said suddenly. "What's happening to my mask?"

Ben looked down to see Mr. Hartman's chin pro-truding from the woolen ski mask. The stitching was unraveling from the bottom on up!

"Oh, no!" exclaimed Savannah. "It's caught on something! There!" She pointed back down the hall.

Ben wheeled. A single strand of yarn marked their passage all the way along the corridor.

"Stop!" ordered Mr. Hartman as his nose was revealed. "I can't let the cameras see me!"

"Where are the brakes on this thing?" Ben wailed. Desperately, he stuck out a foot in an effort to halt the rolling chair.

It was a mistake. The front-most wheel ran over his toe.

"Ow!"

That was when he lost his grip on the chair back. Ben and Savannah watched in horror as Mr. Hartman rolled down the hall, still belted to the freewheeling swivel chair. He careened past the elevator and disappeared through a door at the end of the corridor.

Ben took in the sign above it: STAIRWELL A.

The stairs!

30

It was hard to decide which was louder, the crashing or the yelling.

Ben and Savannah sprinted through the stairwell door and stared down, almost too frightened to look. There on the landing below was the wreckage of the chair. Perched atop what had once been the seat was Ferret Face, a piece of torn seat belt still in his little teeth.

Ben's breath caught in his throat. "Where's Mr. Hartman?" His eyes followed the strand of yarn. It led past the landing and around the corner down the next flight.

"Well, what are you waiting for?" came Mr. Hartman's voice. "We've got to get out of here. Now that the power's back on, it's only a matter of time before the government realizes there's something wrong!"

Ben raced down the steps, pausing only long enough to scoop Ferret Face under his collar. Savannah was right behind them. They caught up with Mr. Hartman and pounded to the main floor. Mr. Hartman broke the yarn while he still had half a ski mask in place; Ben and Savannah made sure to keep their T-shirts high on their faces.

Griffin, Pitch, and Logan were waiting impatiently in the reception area.

"What took you so long?" Griffin demanded. "What part of 'hurry up' don't you understand?"

Savannah took the Hover Handler from Pitch's arms. "I'm so happy we have it back!"

They ran outside and headed across the compound toward Route 31. The neighborhood was still dark. The emergency power did not extend past Facility 107-B. By the light pole, they could make out the quiet whir of the SH-9 vacuum cleaner.

Griffin reached for the access gate in the fence.

"Freeze!" Pitch yelled suddenly.

Griffin turned to her quizzically. "What? Why?"

Pitch took out her water bottle and aimed a splash at the door handle. The tiny sparks appeared once more. "The electricity is on! That means the fence is live!"

"I hear the hum," Logan confirmed.

"We're trapped!" breathed Ben.

Mr. Hartman pulled off what was left of his stocking cap, wrapped it around his hand, and reached for the handle. But as soon as he grasped it, a shock sent him jumping back.

"This is bad, Griffin," Pitch said edgily. "How are we going to get past that fence?"

Ben turned to his best friend. "What are we going to do?"

Griffin was pale but calm. "There's nothing we can do," he told them evenly.

"You said you can do anything if you have the right plan!" Logan pleaded.

Griffin shook his head. "Sometimes what you're up against is just too much. Face it, guys. We gave it our best shot. And we found the Hover Handler. But that's as far as we're going to get."

"Then the government wins!" Mr. Hartman protested.

That was when they heard the sirens in the distance — not just one; a symphony.

"Cops!" Ben exclaimed in agony.

Griffin took out his phone. "I guess it's time to call our folks," he said resignedly. "They'd better know we're probably going to get arrested."

"Not yet!" commanded Savannah. "Stand back, everybody! There's no way I'm letting down Luthor and Melissa over something as puny as an electric fence!"

She set the Hover Handler on its base a few feet in front of the gate and switched it on. Then she reached into her pocket and pulled out Luthor's old collar, the one that still had a GPS transmitter on it.

"Savannah," Griffin spoke up, "what are you —?"

Before he could finish, the girl reared back and hurled the collar with all her might. It sailed over the fence and into the middle of Route 31. To Melissa's Hover Handler, this could only mean one thing: A dog had run out into the road and needed to be lured to safety.

The four rotor blades whirled to life, and the Hover Handler lifted off the base. It made a direct line for the collar, smashing into the gate and knocking it wide open in a shower of sparks.

Savannah snatched up the base. *"Now!"* And she led the way through the fence.

The Hover Handler hovered at an odd angle, one rotor broken off. Lopsided, it hung there over the collar, emitting its high-pitched tone, the one that always set Luthor dancing.

"Savannah, you're a genius!" Griffin praised. "You saved the plan!"

No sooner were the words out of his mouth than a taxi came along Route 31 and squashed the collar — and the GPS transmitter attached to it — flat as roadkill.

As the taxi drove away, the wail of the sirens returned, growing louder.

With no signal to home in on, the damaged Hover Handler began to wobble in an aimless loop, spiraling higher and higher above them.

"What's it doing?" asked Logan, alarmed.

"It needs some place to go! Put the base down!" Griffin ordered.

Savannah set the stand on the sidewalk and reversed a half-step. The group looked up into the night, to see if the wounded Hover Handler would return home.

And it did. The unit stopped its climb and started its descent, gaining speed.

"It's coming in too fast!" Pitch shouted.

Everybody jumped backward.

CRASH!

Melissa's invention slammed into its base at terminal velocity, shattering into a million pieces. Wires, springs, and shards of metal and plastic pelted the five team members and Mr. Hartman.

When the dust cleared, the device and its base were gone, replaced by a wide scatter of debris. Even Ferret Face looked on in awe.

"I don't think Melissa could fix that," Logan observed. "You know, if there was any way we could gather it all up."

Pitch shrugged. "Well, we have a vacuum cleaner . . . I'm joking!" she added when they all glared at her.

Savannah was close to tears. "I can't believe it's gone! Poor Luthor! Poor Melissa!"

"This is how our government works," said Mr. Hartman bitterly. "We've got a handful of smashed-up junk, but the CIA probably has a secret factory hidden away somewhere, turning these things out by the hundreds."

"Along with a new batch of seat-belt chairs," said Ben pointedly.

Now there was nothing distant about the sirens. At this range, the team members could make out the whine and blurp of several different squad cars. The police were coming — a lot of them. And soon.

"Code Z!" Griffin called.

The team sprang into action. Every operation had a Code Z. It meant that the plan had to be abandoned, and pronto.

The instant Griffin yanked the SH-9 free from the wiring of the streetlight, the neighborhood around Facility 107-B began to flicker back to life. Businesses' neon signs glowed once more. The barber pole resumed its rotation. The clock in front of the bank came on again, forty-seven minutes behind.

The team helped Griffin cram the vacuum back into the duffel. At that moment, the Wagoneer wheeled out of the parking lot of Saigon Palace and screeched up to the curb, bringing with it the faint smell of chili oil.

As they pulled away, Griffin peered out the rear window at the flashing lights of the squad cars just over the rise in the road.

Operation Recover Hover, Phase 3, was over.

And there would never be a Phase 4.

31

The Long Island Invent-a-Palooza was being held at Green Hollow High School, not far from Cedarville.

Mr. Bing backed the station wagon up to the loading bay and shut off the engine. "Well," he said, trying to sound encouraging, "here we are."

Griffin had been looking forward to this day like a prisoner awaiting his own eggs-ecution. In the end, Dad had taken pity on him and had labored feverishly alongside his son, trying to work the bugs out of what was now the SH-10. With no success. In an hour, Griffin was going to demonstrate his invention in front of the Invent-a-Palooza judges, and every light in the auditorium was going to go dark.

"Maybe the judges won't mind." His father struggled to find something positive to say. "After all, you really did quiet that motor."

"Yeah," said Griffin glumly. "And maybe the moon will fall out of the sky." He hefted the duffel bag that held his so-called invention. He took a few steps toward the school, and then turned around when he heard the station wagon starting up again. "Aren't you coming?"

"Of course. I'm just going to park the car around the front."

It dawned on Griffin. "You don't want to be seen walking in with me."

His father sighed. "Try to understand. In my world, it's never good to be associated with something that doesn't work, especially when it has such a catastrophic side effect. I can't have people worrying that my inventions might not be reliable."

Griffin nodded sadly. "Yeah, I get it. I'll meet you back at the car after it's all over." He could feel his shoulders slumped a little lower as he carried the SH-10 inside. The one silver lining to the Invent-a-Palooza black cloud was that his father would be there to stand by him. And Dad would, but only from a distance.

"Beep, beep! Championship invention coming through!" The stainless-steel bulk of the EGGS-traordinary bumped past Griffin, nearly causing him to drop his duffel bag. "Oh, hey, Bing. Nice day to get your butt kicked at inventing, huh?"

"Let's go, Darren. We haven't got all day," came Mr. Vader's voice from the other side of the gleaming egg cooker.

"Right, Dad." But before moving on, he leaned over to Griffin and whispered, "Remind me to get you the latest draft of your speech, since you'll be giving it at school on Monday. Hey, how many *O*s are there in *moron*?"

"Yeah, good luck to you, too," Griffin mumbled.

He followed the Vaders through the loading bay, past an equipment locker, and into the large double gym. The Invent-a-Palooza logo was draped across a raised platform at the far end of the room. In front of it, tables had been set up where the young inventors would demonstrate their entries for the judges.

Griffin scanned the audience in search of any friendly face. Nothing. No, there was Dad, climbing to the very last row of bleachers. He was wearing sunglasses and a baseball cap with the brim pulled low. It was better than nothing, but not much better.

And then his eyes fell on another familiar face— the last person he expected to see. He put down his duffel on the table beside his name and walked toward her. By the time he reached her place in the fourth row of bleachers, he was running.

"Melissa, what are you doing here?"

The curtain of hair parted, and the beady eyes peered out. "I came to cheer you on."

"It should be me cheering *you* on," Griffin amended. "Your Hover Handler would wipe up the competition today—you know, if you still had it."

"Pitch and Savannah came over," Melissa went on shyly. "I tried to send them away, but this time my parents made me listen." She looked sheepish. "I'm glad I did. Pitch told me about Operation Recover Hover. All three phases."

"I'm sorry we couldn't get it back for you in one piece." He decided not to mention how many pieces there were by the time the plan was over — probably about fifty thousand.

"I can't believe you did all that for me."

"I was a jerk," Griffin insisted. "I should have had the brains to see that you were the real inventor, not me. But everyone was making a big deal about my dad. And before I knew it, I was in that dumb bet with Vader. And then that boys-versus-girls stuff. It just got out of hand."

"I'm the one who should be saying sorry to you," she countered. "I was so upset when my Hover Handler got stolen that I didn't know how to react. So I kind of shut down. I almost went back to the way things used to be before I started hanging out with you guys. No Hover Handler is worth that." She peered intently at him through a few stray strands of hair. "An invention is just a thing. Friends are way more important."

A compact bundle of gray fur came darting along the bleachers, followed by a hustling Ben. He grabbed Ferret Face by the tail and stuffed him back inside his shirt. "You are *not* going after the candy under the bleachers," he said sternly. "I can't take you anywhere these days."

Behind Ben, Pitch and Logan sidled along to take their seats.

"I didn't think you guys were coming," Griffin commented.

"What are friends for?" Pitch replied. "Savannah's here, too, waiting in the parking lot with Luthor. Turns out, no dogs are allowed inside. She's pretty steamed."

"How's Luthor doing with the shock collar?" Griffin asked.

"He isn't," Logan supplied. "Savannah couldn't go through with it. She bought a regular collar that looks exactly like the shock one, and her parents don't know."

"And does he still chase the exterminator's truck?"

Pitch shrugged. "It's in the shop getting a new transmission, so he hasn't had a chance to yet."

"Hey, listen, Griffin," Ben put in enthusiastically. "Guess what we saw when Mr. Drysdale was driving us over here? Heartless is taking down his fence."

Griffin was not impressed. "Probably so he can put up a bigger one."

"That's what I figured. But when we stopped to ask him about it, he said anyone who's been oppressed by the government is family, and we can cross his property whenever we want to."

"Savannah's dad seemed pretty weirded out," Logan added. "But I think we got our shortcut back, and that's the main thing."

Griffin sighed. "Well, at least something went right out of this whole mess." He glanced at his watch. "I suppose it's time to face the music."

"We'll cheer for you," Ben promised. "Even if we have to do it in the dark."

"Save your breath," Griffin advised. "If you really want to help me, find a person with a decent invention and cheer like crazy for them. I'm a lost cause, but maybe — just maybe — there's somebody who can beat Vader and get me out of that speech!"

The judging began, school by school. Cedarville Middle School was up last.

Great, Griffin thought bitterly. *Prolong the agony. Make it last.*

As the inventions were introduced, one by one, Griffin's heart sank farther into his sneakers. The other contestants were smart kids, but their entries were either lame gimmicks or recycled science fair projects. There was a pocketbook with a built-in interior light, a go-kart that ran on used French-fry grease, a smartphone app that organized all your other smartphone apps, a Santa-themed electric train that ran on a track that would circle your Christmas tree, a sharpener for meat scissors, a Foucault pendulum that wasn't an invention at all, except by Foucault himself a hundred and sixty–odd years ago, and on and on and on.

It was painful, but he couldn't stop himself from looking over at the gleaming form of Darren's EGGStraordinary. There was no chance for anybody else. Not that Darren had much part in creating it, beyond eating the finished product.

A faint bark from outside the school reached his ears, and an insane plan began to form in Griffin's mind. If he could somehow get Luthor in here to trash the Invent-a-Palooza, the paramedics might have to call off the competition before he had to present the SH-10. He even gave it a name—Operation Prevent-a-Palooza. It might have worked, too, if he'd had the foresight to get Savannah on board.

"And now we move on to the final school of the competition, Cedarville Middle," declared the PA announcer. *"We begin with Darren Vader presenting the EGGS-traordinary."*

It was a thousand times worse than Griffin had anticipated, which made it very bad indeed.

A few minutes into the egg-cooking performance, steaming plates were rolling along the conveyor belt and into the hands of the judges for sampling. The audience, which had been pretty bored the whole time, began to come alive, breaking into applause and cheers as each new dish made its appearance. Chef Darren, Invent-a-Palooza's darling, basked in the adulation of the crowd and never missed a chance to toss a leer in Griffin's direction.

Darren wasn't just going to win this competition; they were probably going to crown him king.

Griffin's eyes locked with Ben's in the bleachers. His friend wore an expression of deep sympathy.

"And our last entrant of the day is Griffin Bing with his invention, the SH-10."

There was a smattering of applause, but most of the audience was still watching Darren, who was continuing to churn out egg dishes from his wondrous machine. Now he was loading his creations onto paper plates and passing them into the audience.

"Uh—hi, everybody. My name is Griffin Bing. Have you ever asked yourself why motors on vacuum cleaners and other small appliances have to be so loud?" His voice sounded alien, high-pitched and unfamiliar, as it echoed around the big gym.

In the fourth row, Logan was tapping under his chin, directing Griffin to speak up, to project. Griffin ignored him. He didn't care if he was heard or not. First of all, hardly anyone was paying attention; and second, once the SH-10 did its thing, nobody was going to care.

"I invented the SH-10 to prove that motors don't have to make so much noise. This vacuum used to create an unbearable racket, and listen to it now."

He plugged the power cord into the outlet on the gym floor, shut his eyes, and hit the switch.

The machine purred to life with its pleasant hum. The audience didn't respond at all. They couldn't hear it. But the judges looked genuinely impressed with the SH-10's performance—for about a second and a half.

That was when the lights went out.

It wasn't total darkness, because the gym had ceiling-level windows, and the day was sunny. The judges looked on in amazement. They were scientists and university professors. They concluded immediately that the SH-10 was the cause of the power failure. But this could be no ordinary blackout—not when *the vacuum cleaner itself was still running!*

A short distance away, Darren's EGGS-traordinary coughed into auxiliary-battery mode, issued a hollow *thunk*, and shot a raw egg into the crowd. It caught a lady in the sixth row full in the face. She screamed in distress. But by the time attention turned to her, *thunk*, a second egg was airborne. It soon decorated the lapel of the suit worn by the superintendent of the Green Hollow school district. *Thunk! Thunk! Thunk!* Three more eggs shot into the audience.

Now, people were scrambling in all directions. This made very little sense, as there was no way to predict where the next egg was going to land.

Darren's father came racing in from the bleachers, intent on reaching his son's invention. His foot came down in a slimy egg yolk, and he wiped out before ever making it to the floor.

"Somebody stop this crazy thing!" shouted Darren.

But the EGGS-traordinary was just getting started. It began hurling eggs with greater speed, striking faces and retreating backs. Sticky goo flew everywhere, lodging in clothing and hair.

Even Ben got hit, much to the delight of Ferret Face, who thought raw egg was a delicacy.

Melissa's curtain of hair was pushed aside, her eyes wide as she took in the chaos. "Darren's invention seems to be malfunctioning."

"You think?" chortled Pitch, brushing eggshell off her jeans.

Thunk! Thunk! Thunk! Thunk!

The first few spectators reached the exit door and threw it open. They found their way blocked by the largest, meanest-looking Doberman any of them had ever seen. They turned back into the gym, where it was raining eggs.

Thunk! The last egg painted the basketball scoreboard.

Griffin pulled the plug on the SH-10. The lights came back on.

The EGGS-traordinary tried to continue making egg dishes, but it was out of raw material. It short-circuited with a *zap*, belching out a cloud of smoke.

"That wasn't my fault!" Darren said quickly. He turned to the judges, suddenly nervous. "Was it?"

But the judges had eyes only for Griffin.

"Magnificent!" the first man exclaimed.

Griffin stared. "It is?"

"Well, of course it is!" said a woman, a physics professor. "Many great advances are made at least partly by accident, but who could have expected a middle schooler to create an energy damper of such power and efficiency?"

"Remarkable!"

"Astonishing!"

The head judge spoke up again. "We don't even have to look at our scores. There's no doubt in any of our minds that the SH-10 Energy Damper is our winner here. Congratulations, Griffin."

The fourth row erupted in cheers, and so did Mr. Bing at the very back. His baseball cap was off, and he had stashed his sunglasses.

"That's my boy!" he called out.

"What?" Darren raged. "No fair! He didn't win! *I* won!"

Mr. Kropotkin rushed down from the bleachers. Griffin hardly recognized him. He was covered in egg. An unbroken yolk peered out of his hair like a third eyeball. "You did it, Griffin! Congratulations! You're a credit to our school!"

"He's not a credit!" Darren howled. "I'm a credit! He wrecked my invention and made it slime the audience! He should be disqualified! I win!"

"Don't worry, Darren," Griffin said sweetly. "You'll have your moment in the spotlight. I've already started thinking about your speech."

32

As the Long Island champion, Griffin earned the right to exhibit his invention at the New York state finals.

Mr. Bing was only too happy to accompany his son to Saratoga Springs for the competition. He may have been reluctant to associate himself with the vacuum cleaner that turned out all the lights, but the revolutionary new energy damper was a brilliant discovery — at least that was what he posted on the American Inventors Association's list serve.

They checked into their motel and settled down in their room to relax and prepare for tomorrow's early start, sharing a bag of microwave popcorn in front of the TV.

Mr. Bing brushed a few spilled kernels into his palm and dropped them into the wastebasket.

Griffin grinned at his father. "You know, Dad, we *do* have a vacuum cleaner with us."

"Yeah," his father replied, "but I don't think the hotel would appreciate being plunged into darkness."

He grew serious. "I want you to know how proud I am of you. It's a huge thing for a man to see his kid follow in his footsteps."

Griffin laughed. "We both spent weeks trying to get all those SHs to *not* turn off the power. It's just sheer luck that an energy damper turns out to be a real thing. If the quiet motor had worked the way we wanted it to, it would be Vader in this hotel room, not me."

"No way," his father deadpanned. "The Vaders would be at the Four Seasons, having caviar instead of popcorn."

"But you know, Dad," Griffin went on, "even though I'm not a real inventor, I've learned so much about what you do, and how hard it is. When I look at a SmartPick, I kind of take it for granted, because it's been around for so long. But that thing never existed until you thought of it. It's really amazing."

Mr. Bing was all choked up. "Thanks, Griffin. That means a lot. Now we should probably hit the hay."

"Not yet. I promised Logan I'd watch the ten o'clock news. His new commercial is scheduled to premiere during the first break."

Father and son shared a pretty good laugh over Logan's agonized *"Yeow!"* as his regular bandage was ripped from his skin, and his happy *"Mmmm!"* when the process was repeated with the Ouch-Free brand. Both Bings applauded in the small room as the ad ended and the news anchor reappeared on the screen.

"Our next story comes to us from Limestone,

Maine, where the air force has always had a problem with the local moose population wandering onto the runways of the Loring Strategic Air Command Base. Until now, that is. Air force officials report that the new Runway Ranger keeps unwanted visitors clear of the tarmacs with a ninety-five percent success rate. Have a look."

The video showed a huge moose wandering on an expanse of runway, surrounded by the north woods. Suddenly, the enormous animal leaped up on its hind legs and began a strange lumbering rhythmic motion, its front hooves raised and pumping.

Griffin gawked. He goggled. He blinked, and blinked again. But it was still there—a giant moose in the throes of the very same hip-hop dance that Luthor had always done when the Hover Handler emitted its high-pitched tone!

And then the camera zoomed in on the cause of this peculiar behavior.

The military's new Runway Ranger hovered over the gyrating antlers. It looked like a silver cable box topped by an X-shaped superstructure, and four miniature rotor blades.

"It's a Hover Handler!" Griffin shrieked.

"A what?" Mr. Bing queried.

"Melissa's Invent-a-Palooza project! They were using it to keep Luthor from chasing the exterminator's truck! And then it got stolen! Now we know why! So the air force could turn it into the Runway Ranger!"

His father was skeptical. "I'm sure it's similar, but I really don't think—"

"It's not similar! It's exactly the same! I can't believe they did this! Our own government is out of control! How can we sit back and watch while they . . ." His voice trailed off when he realized how much he sounded like Mr. Hartman.

The next thing you know, I'll be digging a secret shelter under our basement!

Griffin sighed. There was no way he could ever explain all this to Dad—not without revealing how the team had used the SH-9 to break into Facility 107-B. And that was something none of their parents must ever find out.

"I know Melissa's really bright," Mr. Bing went on. "But inventing is a funny game. Who's to say that, while I was developing the SmartPick, there wasn't some guy on the opposite side of the world working on exactly the same idea? If he'd finished and patented first, all my hard work would have been for nothing. Some of the greatest inventors in history never get any credit at all for their creations."

Griffin was still upset. "Even in a total rip-off like this?"

His father nodded. "You have to be satisfied that you've done your part to make the world a better place. For a true inventor, everything else is just gravy."

The envelope had no return address and was post-marked Washington, DC. Melissa turned it over in her hand. Who did she know in Washington? The stationery inside had no letterhead, and the message itself was handwritten.

Dear Miss Dukakis,

I am Major General Steven B. McAllister, in command of the New Electronics Development for the United States Air Force. You may be aware that we have borrowed the technology built into our new Runway Ranger from the design by you. Your government is grateful.

I am not authorized to offer you financial compensation, nor official recognition. In fact, if you show this letter to anyone, the air force will denounce it as a forgery.

However, tech guy to tech guy, what you have accomplished at such a young age is simply genius. The government needs people like you, Melissa Dukakis. I'm offering you a job the instant you graduate from college. Rest assured that you will hear from my department on that very day.

Yours truly,
General Steven B. McAllister
The Pentagon

A tiny smile blossomed behind her curtain of hair. She fed the page into a scanner. An instant later, it appeared on the screen of every device in her room. Then she refolded the letter and placed it lovingly in the shoe box where she kept her most prized possessions.

"What was that envelope that came for you?" her mother asked later in the day.

"Oh, nothing," she replied. "Just junk mail."

It would be her secret, at least until college graduation.

A ttention everybody. I have a little—uh—speech to make."

Darren Vader, his round face tomato-red, stood at the front of the cafeteria atop the small platform teachers used for important announcements. Although he was speaking into a microphone, he was mumbling so quietly that most of the students never even looked up from their lunches.

That suited Darren just fine. This was a speech he very much didn't want to give.

At their first-row table, Ben nudged Griffin. "Doesn't it figure? Most of the time you can hear his big mouth from the International Space Station. And today of all days, he develops an 'inside voice.'"

Pitch cupped her hands to her mouth. "Louder, Darren!"

"Project!" added Logan, tapping his throat in a theater gesture.

Savannah and Melissa looked on, basking in enjoyment. For the first time ever, Melissa had tied back her curtain of hair so she wouldn't miss anything. Even Ferret Face peered out from Ben's sleeve, taking in the spectacle of Darren's humiliation.

". . . Well—uh—maybe you heard that Bing did a teeny bit better than me at the Invent-a-Palooza. So"—Darren's face twisted—"congratulations . . ."

"You let him off too easy," Ben told Griffin. "If it was me, I would have taken the speech Vader gave you and switched the names around."

Griffin shook his head. "Then I'd be no better than him."

". . . Cedarville is proud of you, Griffin. Your invention was great. Mine was—uh—less great. . . ."

"That's supposed to be 'a menace to society,'" Griffin called out sternly. "Follow the script, Vader!"

Pitch stood up. "Can I have that last part again? About how Griffin won and you went down in flames?"

By this time, Darren was babbling. ". . . and—uh—way to go, Griffin . . . you're the—uh—better man . . ." Suddenly, his face darkened to an unhealthy shade of purple, and he bellowed, *"because you totally lousy-stinking cheated!"*

Everybody jumped. Darren's amplified voice reverberated off the cafeteria walls. He had 100 percent attention now.

"It's *not fair* that Bing won with a broken vacuum cleaner! And when he turned it on, it broke *my* project, which was *a thousand times better*! The whole Invent-a-Palooza is a big *scam*! I got *ripped off . . .* !"

As Darren went on raving, Griffin addressed his team. "Would someone care to do the honors?"

"It should be you," Ben decided for the group. "You've earned it."

Griffin reached over and plugged the cord of his SH-10 into the wall socket.

"The judges were all morons!" Darren was booming. *"The fix was in—!"*

The lights went out, the fans stopped, the ice cream freezer fell silent, and the microphone went dead. Darren was still ranting away, but no one could hear what he was saying.

The cafeteria crowd leaped to its feet in a mock standing ovation.

Griffin smiled in deep satisfaction. He'd never cared much about the SH-10 before, but if it shut up Darren Vader, then it really was an invention that could make the world a better place.

Maybe Griffin was following in Dad's footsteps after all.

After school, Savannah walked Luthor down Honeybee Street, enjoying the sunshine of a brisk day. It was the kind of weather the Doberman liked best, and he was all over the place at the end of the long leash, chasing leaves, investigating birds, and rubbing his long body against the trunks of trees.

The big dog wasn't just a free spirit. He appreciated the simple things that made life worthwhile. If only humans could have Luthor's positive attitude.

Honeybee Street looked so much more welcoming now that Mr. Hartman had taken down his awful fence. He wasn't heartless at all, once you got to know him a little. Sure, he was a little strange, always whispering ominous warnings like "The walls have ears" and "They don't know that we know." He definitely still had a serious hang-up about the government. But he was friendly now.

There he was, outside his house, laying down a gravel path on the shortcut he had given back to them.

She waved. "Looking good, Mr. Hartman."

And he stage-whispered back, "Trust no one!"

At the sound of the backfire, Luthor stiffened, and so did Savannah. She grasped the leash with both hands. If this was what she thought it was, she was going to have to hold on. It had been so nice when the truck from Ralph's Exterminators had been in for repair. She wasn't expecting him back on the road until next week. Why hadn't Ralph warned her?

The exterminator rounded the corner into view, and Luthor let out a bark that rattled the treetops. Birds flapped for parts unknown. Savannah tightened her grip on the lead.

"Calm down, Sweetie," she said in her best dog-whisperer voice.

The truck backfired again, and Luthor was gone, the leash blasting out of her hands. Savannah knew with a sinking heart that five of her could not have held him back.

Luthor bounded up the center line, on a collision course with the red truck. This time he didn't have to catch it; it was coming right for him.

"Luthor—no!" Savannah wailed.

As she scrambled after her beloved dog, she could clearly see Ralph behind the wheel, his face a mask of sheer terror. Suddenly, the exterminator slammed on the brakes, threw open the door, and hit the road running.

The former guard dog left his feet in a titanic leap. He sailed through the air and landed on all fours on top of the hood of the truck.

In spite of her agitation, Savannah was fascinated. One of the age-old questions of animal behavior was what would a dog do with the car he was chasing if he ever caught it?

The world was about to find out.

Luthor opened a gaping mouth and clamped it down on the mouse hood ornament. Savannah could see the muscles bulging in his neck as he pulled. He worried it like a shark clamped on to a fighting tarpon until the mechanism broke and the piece came out in his mouth. Then he hopped down to the road, trotted back to Savannah, and deposited the silver mouse, drool-covered and slightly mangled, at her feet.

Proudly, he looked up at her and waited for the gratitude and love that he knew he was entitled to.

Well, what do you know? she thought to herself. *All he wanted was to give me a present.*

Luthor never chased the exterminator's truck again.